M I M I

MIMI

LEE MORELL

CUTTING EDGE

ISBN-13: 978-1-952138-56-0

Published by
Cutting Edge Books
PO Box 8212
Calabasas, CA 91372
www.cuttingedgebooks.com

ONE

S HE GRIPPED the microphone and crooned the lyrics of the sultry song. The house was dark and the spotlight gave her skin a silvery warmth. She looked like a tiny kewpie doll with her lush curves and dimpled loveliness. Her large violet eyes were half hidden under heavy lids. She was in a trance, swaying slightly in rhythm to the musical backing Griff was giving her.

She was on fire and had the audience, as she always did, on the edge with her, pulsing, feeling what she felt, hungering for what she hungered, aching where she ached. She was aching and hungering now. She could feel her pointed breasts throbbing and swelling against the fllmsy silk evening gown. A sharp pain was inching down her thighs which were spread wide apart and pressing hard toward the wooden floor.

She always felt this way when she sang with Griff's backing. It was magic. It reached out and grabbed all who were near. She could not sing unless her whole being was on fire, a living flame consuming itself in its ravenous hunger.

She was hungry—hungry for Griff, wanting to be held by him, to feel his fingers exploring her eager body, his lips seeking hers and finally crushing them in a burst of desire. Without him, she would be unable to sing; part of her would be dead forever. She sighed into the song, and her listeners sighed right back. The band backed her hard and Griff came in for a brief solo. The house went wild.

Then, just as she turned the last chorus, she saw them—the Thorntons. She had known they were coming—Griff had told her—and yet, when she saw the tall, thin man with the pretty woman in the wheelchair enter the room, she realized that she had not actually believed him. Mimi concentrated on the song's lyrics but her huge violet eyes held the couple for a long moment.

The headwaiter was keeping them at the door until she finished the number. She was conscious of the rapt, upturned faces of the audience and she felt Griff's eyes on her back, boring hard. She turned ever so slightly toward him. His cheeks bulged and his fingers worked the stops of the clarinet with his own magic, making noodles above her voice for the finale. For one fleeting second, her wide-set violet eyes blazed with unrestrained abandon. Then it was over.

She started for the stairs that led from the platform to the floor below, her spike heels clacking on the wooden floor, her hips swinging insolently and fluidly. As she reached the stairs, Griff's arm grasped her firmly.

"Get this, kid!" he hissed in her ear. "You've got to play this straight, see? This might be our big break. After all, what have we got to lose? We're broke, remember?"

"Griff, I just don't get it. I don't give a damn about the money that's involved. How you let that Thornton woman talk you into even considering this deal is one for the books. I think you're off your rocker completely."

"Now look," he spat at her. "They've got a proposition that makes sense. It's a natural. If you goof it, we're through for good. For good, you understand?"

She looked at him in horrified disbelief.

"I tell you," he said emphatically, "this could mean all the difference to us between the big time and more of this goddam grubbing. It's up to you. All you've got to do is spend nine months bearing a kid for them—and what's that to you?—and then, baby, we're in the dough. You and me, money in the bank and freedom to tell the world to go blow. What could be more simple?"

"Oh, Griff, no," she said despairingly.

"Oh, Mimi, yes," he mocked, giving her a small but firm shove.

By the time she reached the table, the Thorntons were seated and had given their order to the waiter. She stood before them and openly eyed them with arrogance and disdain. Her face was a set mask in which only the violet eyes burned. The man's gray eyes rose to meet hers. For a tense second their glances interlocked and then a slow flush rose painfully to his cheeks.

Mrs. Thornton smiled at her. "Do sit down, Miss Vanguaard. You sing so beautifully, Another moment and I think I would have been in tears—and quite unashamed."

Mimi stared at her and said nothing. Thornton's long fingers played with his drink delicately. He's embarrassed, Mimi thought. He was a good-looker, all right. He reeked of class and money. She could almost smell the money. She wished she could tell them off, turn on her heels and walk out. Oh, Griff, how could you? Her heart tossed out the question in agony but her lips made no sound and her face remained icily composed.

Mrs. Thornton looked at her with friendly understanding, a soft smile hovering about her mouth. I could like you, Mimi thought. Maybe I could even like you both. Maybe you're okay, but why do you have to come barging in on things like this? As if in answer to her thoughts, Mrs. Thornton leaned toward her. Her voice was warm and vibrant.

"I know what you must be thinking, Miss Vanguaard," she said gently. "You're wondering if Philip—my husband—and I are just completely mad, out of our right minds. Please hear us out before you jump to any conclusions."

Mimi remained immobile, expressionless and aloof. Philip Thornton stirred uneasily. It's not his idea at all, it's hers, Mimi thought with surprise. How odd.

"The Thorntons are a family of great tradition," Leyra Thornton began. "There have been Thorntons out in our Long Island home, Forest Green, for longer than anyone can remember. We hope there shall be many more for generations to come. However, we—Philip and I—are without children. As you can see, I am an invalid." She hesitated and bit her lip. Sorrow etched fleeting lines in her face. "I can never give Philip an heir."

Leyra sipped her drink but her eyes, searching and intent, never left Mimi's face. During this time her husband had not lifted his eyes from his drink. Mimi gazed at him anew. She took in the tall, lanky form—taller than Griff's six feet—and the polished manners. His pale skin matched his sandy hair and gray eyes, and the sharply chiseled features had a rare purity that she found intriguing. Looking at the ripe and sensual mouth, Mimi felt a slight tremor ripple through her.

"Of course," Leyra continued persuasively, "we are prepared to remunerate you well and to take care of all expenses."

Her voice caught a little and she became silent. The man's well-shaped hand left his drink, found his wife's hand on the table and covered it with his own. Mimi didn't miss the catch in the voice nor the movement of the hand. He's gone on her! she thought. He cares for her and yet he would do this thing.

"Why don't you adopt a child?" Her question was impersonal and cold.

"We've thought of that," Leyra said quickly, "but an adopted child is not quite like one's own flesh and blood—and our lawyer feels that there might be legal problems later about the inheritance."

Again, robot-like, Mimi questioned. "What happened to you?" She indicated the wheelchair.

Leyra flushed but answered with a trace of pride. "I was thrown from my horse and my spine was injured permanently." She waited for some comment, then continued as none was forthcoming. "I was with child when I fell. That was to be my last ride until—" She broke off again. "Well, it was at that, I guess, my last ride."

She was silent for a moment as the orchestra gave a crescendo that thundered through the close room. When she spoke again, there was a new, imploring ring in her voice.

"This is very crucial to us, Miss Vanguaard. I can't tell you how crucial. I—"

At this out-and-out plea, Mimi's control broke. Rage flooded through her like an electric shock. "Do you really think I care?" she exploded. "What do you think I am—a two-bit hustler? How could you dare to think I—"

She felt a heavy hand on her shoulder. "Hi ya, kitten! Evening, folks! How do you like the music? Everything all right?"

She should have known that Griff would follow her, that he wouldn't trust her. The pressure of his fingers bore down hard on her shoulder.

"Griff, you already know Mrs. Thornton, I believe. This is Mr. Philip Thorton. Griff Stamm, the leader of our band."

Griff smiled at Leyra with a twinkle in his eye and then extended his hand to Philip. "Glad to meet you, sir."

He bent to Philip with just the proper amount of deference. "May I join you for a moment?" He beckoned to the waiter as he sat down at the urgings of the Thorntons who, Mimi saw, were quickly responding to the easy Griff charm.

"How do you like the Paradise Club? This place is usually jammed—and I mean packed like sardines. Nice crowd tonight but ordinarily reservations are the only way in." He turned and smiled brightly. "If you should ever have trouble that way, I'd be glad to help out. Any time."

He was apple-polishing, easily, smoothly. And no one could resist the crooked smile or the casual approach. Mimi watched the Thorntons fall for it. Her hands fluffed her hair tensely.

"Miss Vanguaard and I have been here for some time now," Griff went on. "We play at some private engagements now and then—but generally this place keeps us so on the go that we haven't been getting out much lately."

Leyra looked at her husband with sparkling eyes. "Dear why don't we invite them to play at your birthday party next week?"

Philip Thornton smiled and nodded. Leyra turned to Griff and Mimi. "We would be so glad if you both could come—and bring the band—to entertain at my husband's birthday party next Saturday. We've asked a few friends in. Would it be possible?" Then her face clouded. "Oh, I don't suppose you can. That's your busy day. You'll be needed here that night."

Griff smiled reassuringly. "Don't bet on that. Nick owes us some time. I think I can get him to let us off. I can get some other men to fill in here for us."

"It would be so wonderful if you could come! I'd love to have our friends hear you and Miss Vanguaard. You two are such a wonderful team. And please, try to arrange to stay the weekend."

"Will do. And thanks for the invitation. We'll try to live up to your expectations."

"My husband will have a chauffeur meet you and your men at the station."

"Great. Great. That's wonderful," Griff responded warmly.

Suddenly Philip stood up and grasped Leyra's wheelchair.

"I'll have one of the waiters do that for you if you like, Mrs. Thornton."

"No thank you. I can manage."

The refusal could have been curt but it was not. However, it succeeded in discouraging further offerings. Leyra's gay laughter tinkled. "My husband loves to push me around, Mr. Stamm. We'll see you next week."

Watching the Thorntons leave, the smile remained on Griff's lips but the light in his eyes was cold. He sucked in his cheek and pulled at his lower lip.

"You were going to gum that deal, kitten. I know it. You were going to gum it!"

Mimi's lower lip pouted. "I told you, Griff, it's insane!"

"It's not for you to think. I'll do the thinking. Just do like I tell you. What's in that pretty head anyway—rocks? How long do you think we can go from two-bit clubs to one-night stands? This is our big chance, kitten. This is it!"

"We're doing all right here!"

"Yeah, but for how long? You never know when we'll get kicked out on our tails. And that reminds me—Nick sent word by Silky that he wants to see me."

"Oh, no! I thought we could go off early by ourselves," she wailed.

Griff pulled at his lip. "C'mon. Let's go look for him. He must be in his office downstairs now."

"You know Nick doesn't like for anyone to break up his fun downstairs," she said.

"Well, this is one time I'm gonna break it up. I want to know what this is all about." He grabbed her hand and yanked her to her feet.

"Griff! I've got to put some make-up on before my next number."

"You've plenty of time. Let 'em dance a while."

They wove their way through the closely packed tables to a narrow hall leading to the rear of the Club. The floors were heavily carpeted, muffling the sound of their steps. Here even the music coming from the inner room had lost its harsh blare. Mirrors along the length of the wall threw their images back at them in weird, eerie shapes. At last they came to a short flight of steps leading down. Stretching on each side of a passage at the bottom of the stairs was a row of doors.

Mimi opened her dressing-room door with the large silver star on it and spoke to Griff over her shoulder. "At least let me fix up a minute, please, honey?"

"Oh, all right. But don't take long. Just to make sure, I'll come along with you. I want you with me when I talk to Nick. You have a hell of an effect on that guy!"

The room was decorated as luxuriously as the rest of the Paradise Club. A low sofa was set against the wall facing a brightly lit dressing table. A thick red carpet covered the floor.

Mimi gave Griff a little push that sent him flopping on the sofa. "You stay there, ya big dope, while I fix my face." She went to the dressing table and stared into the mirror.

"That's not fixing your face, kitten. We don't have all night, you know."

"I know. Griff, do we have to go through with this Thornton deal? I just don't want to. I'm no animal in a barn put in the world just to have babies for other people!"

"Oh, for Pete's sake! How many times do I have to explain this set-up to you?" He got up restlessly and bounded over to her. He grasped her shoulders and shook her. "This is for us, kid. For us, you and me. So we can be on Easy Street for the rest of our lives. No more crummy hotels on the road. No more starving in sleazy joints. No more Paradise Clubs." He stood away from her and walked about excitedly, tugging at his lip. "We can go somewhere and open up a club of our own. Yeah, or retire in South America or anyplace with that kind of dough. Grow up, kitten, grow up!"

"It makes me feel horrible," Mimi said miserably. "I wouldn't mind it if it were our baby. I'd love it, but—"

"Oh, there you go again! How many times do I have to tell you? Doesn't fifty thousand bucks mean anything to you at all?"

Mimi shook her head until her curls danced wildly. He held her then and she clung to him. She could feel the hot tears flowing down her cheeks.

"Oh, Griff! It would be different if we were already married. I wouldn't mind it quite so much then."

He tensed; then a second later he was on his knees beside her. "I'll tell you what, kitten. You go through with this thing and we'll be married as soon as it's over."

She looked at him through her tears. "Honest, Griff? You mean it? You mean it this time?"

"I mean it, so help me!"

"You've said that before. But I guess we can go to the party Saturday. I'll make up my mind then about the deal. But do you really mean it now, honey? If I go through with this, we can get married?"

"I swear it. Honest, kitten. This time I mean it."

"Well, kiss me now then, just to prove you really mean it."

"Aw, kitten. You're not gonna stop there and we got to see Nick. It must be something really important."

"It won't take long, Griff. Just love me a little." Her eyes shone soft and misty.

"I know you, kitten, We don't have time."

But she clung to him and dragged him down beside her and fastened her lips to his. He resisted, immobile at first. Then, as her tongue flickered and explored tantalizingly, he came to life with a jerk.

He could feel the hardened tip darting here and there, reaching and exploring, searching the inside of his mouth feverishly. In spite of himself, he relaxed and yielded to the wild surging she always aroused in him. She tugged at his clothing and moved over, making room for him. He trembled as the pink tip wiggled its way deep. He could feel tremor after tremor shake her. Her voice came to him, husky and warm in his ear.

"Please, honey. Please! Please!"

He bent his head low on her throat to nibble at the luscious whiteness revealed by the low-cut evening gown. She fumbled for a moment and suddenly the warm heaviness of her breast was caressing his cheek, its tip hard and erect, jabbing him into a frenzy. There was business to be attended to but this urgency was undeniable. He couldn't leave it now.

Eagerly he made a pilgrimage of her loveliness. And her hands roamed over his body—seeking, always seeking. And in his consciousness something flared like an arc lamp and burned fiercely for a few fleeting seconds. Then, just as quickly, it was extinguished.

He sat up and lit a cigarette, trying to still his seething emotions, There was still work to be done. He was a man on the make. That was enough for the kitten tonight, he told himself. He could not face the truth that even as his passion had reached fever pitch, it had abated, gone flat and insipid. It was always like this when he was with a girl. The idea of conquering was always far more exciting and satisfying than the act itself, which—he knew—should be the climax of joy.

Mimi lay on the sofa, tossing and writhing. He knew he had not spent enough time with her. But that could wait.

"C'mon, kitten. Go wash your face and freshen your make-up. Let's go find Nick."

She lay and whimpered without answering. He bent over and kissed her cheek lightly. She grasped him about his neck and clung. He tried to undo her fingers.

"We haven't got time tonight! Later, baby. Later. Daddy has got work to do."

"No. Just kiss me once more," she pleaded.

"And start that all over again? Oh, no, baby. I know you!"

"You don't love me, Griff." She sat up. "I don't think I'll go on with this deal."

"Oh, c'mon. Have a heart! We're working tonight, kid. Remember? Afterwards we can—"

"Oh, you always have an excuse," she said peevishly.

There was a loud knock on the door. "Who is it?" Mimi called out.

"It's me! Silky. Nick wants to see Griff right away," a soft, feminine-sounding voice answered.

Griff jumped up. "I knew it!" He stared at her. "I told you, baby. Nick Bothio waits on nobody. And I mean nobody. C'mon!"

Mimi jumped up quickly, hurriedly combed her hair and put on fresh make-up. Together they went out of the room and to the end of the hall where an elevator was waiting. The car took them to a lower floor. Here they were in a different world. There was in reality a separate club below the public nightclub above to which only the specially invited, the elite, the voluptuaries, the sensualists, were admitted. The Place was reserved especially for patrons who enjoyed satisfying their sensual appetites in exotic and bizarre ways.

They stepped out of the elevator into a dimly lit hall. Nick Bothio, the strange, enigmatic, guiding figure behind the Paradise Club and its less-publicized nether domain, was waiting.

TWO

THE PART of the Paradise Club known as The Place was a sensualist's paradise. It was a Never-Never Land for those connoisseurs of pleasure who came seeking relaxation and stimulation of a special sort. Here were all the ingredients for tempting the physical appetite. Its numerous and intimate rooms were arranged in a gigantic circle, each one radiating from a fabulous suite which made up Nick Bothio's offices and personal apartment.

His suite included a carpeted, exotically decorated room and a private bath in which mirrors and shiny, sparkling tiles reflected back one's image from every angle. The bedroom was richly furnished with rare silks and brocades in vivid reds, blues, greens and gold. Velvet and damask draperies hung against one entire wall. On the opposite wall were sparkling mirrors that reached to the ceiling. The only light came from the luminous ceiling, in the center of which was another large mirror.

Directly beneath the ceiling mirror was an immense, circular bed covered with flame-colored velvet. A large cabinet stood against one wall.

As Griff and Mimi approached Nick's private sanctum, they could smell the pungent odor of incense. Mimi's nerves tingled at the very thought of Mr. Nick Bothio. She had heard things of him which frightened and yet fascinated her. As Griff opened the door and held it for her to enter, a vibrant excitement pulsed through her. Bothio was a puzzle to her. No one really knew him—not even the dancer, Asia, who was the closest to him.

Mimi hesitated at the door. Then she heard a soft voice speak from somewhere within the office.

She took a step forward and found herself staring at the tall, dark man facing them. Her nostrils flared at the sight of him and her violet eyes widened. She could not control herself or hide the shock the sight of him, with his blatant ugliness, always gave her.

He smiled as his eyes met hers. Instinctively she knew that he was aware of her fear. The smile itself was scarcely a flicker in the rock-life carving that was his face. A ripple under the surface of a rock of ice, causing it to stir a little—that was all. Then he was walking toward them, hand outstretched in a casual wave.

"Come in. Come in. Sit down and pour your own troubles from the assortment on the table in front of the sofa there." He waved his hand airily. "Or we can go to the bar."

They followed him toward the far wall which, as they approached it, appeared to be nothing but a tiled wall with a huge mosaic of colored stone. In the center of the mosaic was an angry, prancing black horse stamping on a writhing snake. It seemed to Mimi to be a snake but it had a strange shape and an odd pecularity about it. Nick pushed a button and the wall parted and disappeared, revealing a long, well-stocked bar with gleaming bottles and glassware.

Mimi's slim, spike heels sank into the carpet as she moved to the sofa. From there she could see the two men and hear Griff's low, eager voice as he spoke deferentially to Nick.

Presently Nick came over to her with a drink in each hand. "Beauty and the Beast," he said wryly, offering her one of the glasses. "The Beast adoring at the dainty feet of Beauty."

Mimi giggled nervously. "Nick, you say such unexpected things."

"I see," he replied thoughtfully. "You don't think that a hooligan like me reads, eh? That's why you're surprised." He raised his brows archly. "Do you know who my hero was all the time I was in school?"

Mimi shook her head.

"Napoleon," he answered forcefully. "How I adored that man! Even today I still read everything about him I can put my hands on. I used to wish that I had been named after him."

"For a long time I didn't think you had a first name," Mimi told him. "Everybody calls you Bothio."

He nodded. "My first name is Nicholas but if anyone calls me that, I think I'll have him done in right on the spot."

He spoke seriously and the thought of his power brought back her fear of him. She smiled thinly and looked closely at his face when next she dared. Heavy lines ravaged the surface, forming deep ravines from nose to mouth. The lips were beautifully shaped but looked mean and cruel above the jutting chin. His eyes were like black marbles, hard and bright under the bristling, thick brows. The bridge of his nose was sharply aristocratic but his nostrils flared sensually and, as if to confuse, his voice and speech were disarming. The voice was soft, almost caressing. No one had ever heard Bothio raise it. But that soft voice could give deadly commands—commands that could snuff out a life at the snap of his fingers.

Now the voice caressed her as the man's eyes flicked over her, searching, probing and enveloping her in their hypnotic embrace. Mimi shrank. She did not want to get too close to this man.

Bothio knew the very instant that Mimi rejected him. His discernment and acute perception were what gave him his power. It was said that he could always tell when a man was bluffing and correctly call his hand. He was aware that his greatest talent lay in his knowledge of people. Others who knew him said he had a gift for organization. He directed and administered his hoodlum empire like a big business tycoon. No one really knew the extent of his power except himself. He trusted no one—not even Silky, his second in command.

Now he turned to Griff. His manner was crisp and cold. "I want to make you a proposition. You've really been pulling the crowd in. Every night the place is jammed. When Bothio is pleased, he shows his appreciation. When he's sore—" he shrugged.

His hand pulled at the immaculate cuffs at his wrists as he hunched his right shoulder quickly, characteristically.

"I'll tell you about the proposition later. Right now, I want you to work up a production number around Asia. She should have a bigger spot—you know, to do something really spectacular. The kid is a good dancer, yet she's not pulling. So work up something for her, eh? Big. Lush. An exotic number. Show her off. Right?"

At that moment a door at one side of the room opened and a willowy young woman entered the room. She moved with effortless grace toward Bothio. There was a cat-like quality to her walk. Her almond-shaped, green eyes smoldered like burning emeralds. Long red hair cascaded down her back in loose waves and her white face was stark and bare of make-up except for the scarlet slash that was her mouth.

Mimi had seen Asia both on and off the stage before but never as closely as now. She was more than just a little awed by the volcanic dancer who was Bothio's paramour. She had often heard screaming and cursing coming from the dancer's dressing-room, followed by the silky remonstrances of Bothio's major-domo. She never expected to be in the same room with Asia, much less to become friendly with her. Now the girl's sheer sensual power struck her. She knows how to handle Bothio, Mimi thought.

"Will you make that moron, that monkey, keep out of my rooms?" Asia demanded hotly. "He's always under my feet. I'm sick of him." Her voice was heavily accented but Mimi failed to identify its exotic origin.

"Who is it this time?" Bothio demanded mildly. "Somebody is always annoying you, my pet. How can they help themselves?" His eyes raked her. "You're a luscious piece, Asia."

"Stop that!" the girl commanded. "The next time Silky comes into my rooms, I'll crown him, so help me. The freak!"

"I'm sure Silky's intentions are honorable," Bothio murmured soothingly. "They wouldn't dare be otherwise."

Asia turned and, for the first time, caught sight of Mimi curled up on the sofa. "What goes here?" she queried, nodding her head in Mimi's direction.

"I was just talking to Griff about building up your act. Silky went to get you for me—but I don't suppose you gave him a chance to tell you so." A chuckle escaped him. "One of these days you're gonna meet your match, Asia, and I want to be around to see it."

"I can take care of myself," the girl retorted as she tossed her hips saucily. "What's this about my act?"

"I want Griff to write some new music and build up your bit—you know, make a production number, a spectacular, for you," Bothio explained patiently.

"It's about time I got some appreciation around here." Suddenly she turned her enormous cat eyes on Mimi and stared at her impudently. "Maybe I can do a number as background to her singing," she mused, tossing her hips again.

Mimi stirred. Nobody was going to have the stage when she sang except herself, but it would not do to antagonize Asia. She was too close to Bothio.

"I think you ought to have the stage all to yourself when you dance," she said as casually as she could. She sank deeper into the downy cushions and raised her legs against the wall over the sofa so that her dress slipped down to her thighs and teasingly exposed her rounded firmness. She knew the other girl's vanity would be pricked, but before Asia could answer, Griff spoke quickly.

"Mimi's right, Asia. You have the stage to yourself. I can build up your act so it'll really be something to see. You know—music, nice lights to show off the red hair, showgirls in the background, everything."

Mimi hated to see Griff cater to Bothio. She could never understand why he changed so when Bothio was around. It made her flesh crawl to hear the pleading in his voice and to watch the expression in his eyes.

She remembered when she had first met Griff—some two years before in a small beach town in California. It had been a hot, sticky day with the heat beating down in heavy waves. In the beat-up, runabout convertible she had bought from a hot-rodder, she had headed for the beach miles away.

At the time she was singing in the Desert Rat. The band backing her was crummy. None of the men knew music or even how to read it or play it right. Most of them were junkies anyway. Because the Desert Rat was the last spot before the desert, everyone on that route stopped there. There was always some business, but the owners never bothered to build up the place by getting good talent or first-class entertainment.

She had taken the job because the band she had been singing with had folded in Los Angeles and she needed to make her fare back East. But now, on this hot night, she had had it. She was fed up with the cheap junkies and their bad music. She drove the car easily but fast, relishing the coolness of the wind. She soon left the houses behind. The country became wilder and more deserted and the trees took on weird, misshapen outlines. Then, at last, the tangy taste of salt was on her lips and spread before her was the ocean.

She pulled up the car and got out, took off her shoes and stockings and stretched her legs contentedly before her in the sand. After a while she walked along the beach. Suddenly she heard it. Music! In this place! Wonderful music. At first she thought it was a radio. She walked on toward the sound, then stopped suddenly.

A hunched figure was sitting on a rock, blowing his heart out of a licorice stick. She took a step forward, then stopped uncertainly. She made her way to a slight outcropping of rocks where he could not see her. Whoever it was playing the clarinet really knew how that almost impossible instrument should be handled.

She recognized the tune—"How Long Has This Been Going On?"—but he was barely holding to the melody. He was playing with a variation full of riffs and curlicues. Mimi was a good enough musician to recognize the gift when she heard it. And this man had it. He was a musician. A real gone, music-happy stick player. He made a few more fast riffs and headed straight for the high one up in the blue.

She knew it instantly. She could feel deep inside her just what he was going to do next. She did not know how she knew, but she could feel every note he took before he reached for it. Every time he rose up high, before he hit it hard, she knew. She was breathing fast as if she had just run a mile. Her chest hurt. Excitement was bubbling like a boiling volcano inside her. She took a deep breath and closed her eyes tight, shutting out everything—the night, time and the world—everything except the music that was coming at her, shattering her, making her feel like crying, making her want to sing.

Then she was singing—softly, soft-pedaling from way down deep, following along with him. At the sound of her voice the stick player stopped in the middle of a high one. Mimi went on singing, scatting now for the lyrics she forgot. Then the music was coming at her again and she was shaking and scatting and humming, following along, keeping up with him.

He was trying to lose her. He would dip low and then rush high and clean and plunge out to a fast riff. But she held with him. She forgot where she was or who she was or where she came from. Only this mad music was real. The fire inside her was real. She had never sung like this before. Never felt like this before. She had never gone so deep and hadn't even known she had it in her. The only reality left in the world was the music, herself and this man playing the clarinet. Music poured out of her, forced by the player below.

At last he stopped and she awoke from her trance to find that he had walked toward her while he was still playing. He stood beside her. The sound of his voice was like a whiplash.

"Who the hell are you and what the hell are you doing here?" He spoke in the tone a man uses in speaking to a woman he is sure belongs to him.

"I heard the music, so I came."

Her voice was small, and even to herself it sounded used up and far away. She did not look at him. She only wondered what was happening to her until—with a rare flash of insight— she knew. She needed this music-maker, this unknown man. Without looking at him, she knew. She loved him forever—no matter what or how. No matter what he looked like or what he was. He was the only man who could make her feel this way. He was the only man who could make her sing—really sing.

He stood looking down at her for a long minute. She could feel his eyes digging into her in the darkness. Then he settled himself beside her and began to play again. She kept her eyes averted. She did not want to look at him just yet. A strange shyness overcame her and she began to sing again.

That was two years ago. She was still singing. She and Griff had been together ever since. They were a musical team, musically and personally compatible. They were a sensation together. They had shacked up because they wanted to and because it was cheaper to be together. It was convenient on the road, too. Together they had toured the circuit—or wherever they got bookings—and they had stayed together, held fast by music and by an indefinable need for one another.

Griff had managed somehow to get a band together. The men—it was only a small combo, but really good—had stayed because they knew good music and wanted to work with a man who knew more than they did. And Griff did know music. He was a born musician down to his fingertips.

From time to time the combo had changed until now the men left in it were the greatest in the business. As for Mimi, she sang solely because of Griff now. Loving him, wanting him, came out in her music like a hot fever that blistered the skin and parched the throat. Audiences went wild when she sang with Griff backing her. They were really paired—a team, she and Griff.

If only they could get married. But somehow Griff always managed to skitter away when she brought up the idea. She knew he did not love her as she loved him. He was her life, her breath, her dreams. To him, she was a good singer who made great music with him and of whom he was very fond. And sometimes in their most intimate moments, when he was holding her close and time was standing still, she could feel him pull away, reserve a part of himself and leave her even while she clung desperately to him.

She knew there was no other girl. But something stood between them, always keeping them from reaching the full peak of ecstasy. She sensed that was the reason why he did not want to marry her and that he cared for her as much as he could ever care for anyone.

By chance they had landed the job at the Paradise Club. They had been going by—she and Griff in the car and the boys with the instruments in the station wagon—when the music from the Club stopped them. Griff had pulled up to the curb and they had all trooped in. They had liked the spot and Griff left them happily at the bar while he chatted with the bandleader, who told him that he was leaving at the end of the week. The place was too far from town for him. He was on the stuff—a chronic junkie—and had to be near his source of supply.

Griff had unpacked his stick and spelled the leader, who went to shoot stuff in his arm. The audience had gone for it and Griff beckoned Mimi to front with him. Hearing them, Bothio had come out to listen. When they stopped, a contract was wrapped up.

And here they had stayed. They could not get away. Not that they wanted to move on. It was far better than the honky-tonks they had played on the road. If only Griff would marry her, everything would be okay. Perhaps now, if she went through with this Thornton deal, he really would marry her just to get his hands on the $50,000. She smiled wryly. She knew how much he loved money…

She came out of her reverie with a start. They were all looking at her. Griff's voice came to her, soft and cajoling.

"Honey, Nick is inviting us to have supper with him later—after the last show—to discuss Asia's number."

"Sure," Mimi said. "Fine." But her thoughts were not about the invitation. If only Griff would not act so strange when Bothio was around. It was almost as if he, well, liked him—in a way that a man was not supposed to like another man.

She looked at Griff under half-closed eyelids. He was good-looking, all right. Tall and lanky, his sandy hair perhaps too wavy for a man. For the first time she noticed a softness about his face. His large blue eyes, now staring at her, could cloud with feeling as he played. His lips were soft and sensual from puckering and sucking at the stick.

"Oh, Griff!" The cry was wrung out of her. With a leap she crossed the room and clung to him, crying his name over and over again. "Oh, Griff! Griff! No! No!" She pressed her body tight against his. He could feel the heat emanating from her. Her soft belly undulated against his. He pulled at the arms clinging around his neck but could not disengage them without using more force than he wanted to before Bothio. Sweat broke out on his face.

"Mimi! Mimi! Please behave yourself, baby." But she clung to him harder. "What's the matter, baby?"

"Oh, Griff! Griff!" she cried. And Bothio was the only one in the room who understood what she meant.

THREE

MIMI had never before visited Bothio's private apartment. She was prepared for anything except what she saw. The apartment was behind Bothio's office which she and Griff had just passed through. Like everything else in the Paradise Club, it was laid out in the round.

Silky met them at the door. Mimi detested the sight of this slim, smooth-faced man. He was far too beautiful to be a man, she thought. Everything about him revolted her. His long blond hair, which he wore in loose, free-flowing waves, his finely lacquered nails and his mincing ways were sickeningly repugnant to her feminine nature.

And it was the obvious manly strength of his corded, supple muscles playing and rippling under the silken shirts that made her resent his affectations all the more.

Mimi sidled her way past the perfumed and powdered Silky, who was openly smirking at her, and entered a large round antechamber. She could see herself reflected in mirrors no matter where she turned.

"I think you will have to wait a while. Bothio's busy." Silky was openly eyeing Griff. Griff smiled absently and Silky smiled back broadly, winking behind Mimi's back. "I am sure you understand," he twittered as he fluttered away and disappeared behind one of the gleaming mirrors.

Mimi turned to Griff petulantly. "I'm tired, Griff. I don't want to have supper. I just want to go to bed. That last show was a dilly. I thought they'd never stop asking for more, more, more!"

Griff grasped her elbow. "Easy, baby. Easy! The walls have ears. We don't want to spoil anything with Bothio now, do we, kitten?"

She leaned against him, feeling the contours of his muscles. She was beginning to breathe hard so he let her go and she walked about the room, restlessly peering into the mirrors.

In one mirror she saw herself tall and slim as a reed, her buttocks round and large in exaggerated proportions to long, thin legs. She frowned and moved on to another panel. Here she was short and squat, her round breasts floating like great swollen balloons over a slim, skimpy waist and bulbous hips. She moved on quickly and peered into another mirror, and another, until she found one that presented an image acceptable to herself. Then she unashamedly, narcissistically, reveled in the Mimi-image the mirror reflected. She thrilled with pleasure.

One hand rose and caressed first one rounded, ripe breast and then the other. She could feel the nipples hard and erect, straining against her pink gossamer gown. She arched her rounded bottom, making a deep V at the waist as the fabric clung to her lithe form. A dreamy expression was on her face and the dim light cast a warm, pink glow on her flushed cheeks. She looked fresh and moist and sleep-warmed.

Heavy lids lowered over the enormous violet eyes which were glazed with self-love and erotic emotion. Her knees came together slowly as she teetered on the ball of one foot with the heel crossing over to rest on the instep of the other.

Across the room Griff became aware of her, startled by her urgent whimper. From the distance, slim Mimi looked like a graceful Aphrodite poised for flight. As he stared, her tension communicated itself to him and again the almost imperceptible sound, like a sigh, reached him. His skin pebbled as blood rushed to his temples and immediately blotted out all feeling save the rushing torrent of desire that engulfed him.

He was across the room and at her side with one swift swoop. He did not even know he cried her name. "Mimi!" He knew nothing but that he was on his knees beside her and that his hands were clutching the sheer, clinging fabric of her dress. She was taut and rigid, her knees pressed tightly together.

Now she pressed hard against him. Her sigh was a long, drawn-out whisper. Her hands were still cupping her breasts. His head was buried in the folds of the thin garment, lost in its caressing softness. Darkness enveloped him. The woman scent and the perfume she wore smote his nostrils, almost overpowering him.

His body twitched convulsively. Eternal seconds passed while he journeyed far out into another world. Then her hand was on his head, fondling his hair. At last he lifted his face and gazed at her. She seemed to glow with an inner radiant light.

"Oh, Griff! You do love me. Sometimes I think... but now, this minute, I feel that you do love me the same way I love you."

He was on his feet, numbed, the ecstasy of the moment gone, destroyed, he could not say why. He walked over to the sofa and dropped onto it, his face a flaccid white mask as his slender hands smoothed his hair nervously.

Mimi stood where he left her. Mixed emotions etched her face. The transport of passion faded and her violet eyes clouded. Silvery tears cascaded down her cheeks, streaking the faint blush that still lingered. She turned her head and covered her face with her hands, sobbed and rushed blindly toward the side of the room and disappeared through one of the mirrored doors.

She could hear Griff calling her but, blinded by her tears and the despair in her heart, she stumbled along the passageway, not knowing or caring where she went. The passage led to an open door and she stumbled through. A shocking sight stopped her cold.

Bothio was lying spread-eagled on his belly on a narrow canopy bed that was covered with a silken quilt. His hands were tied to iron prongs in the wall behind his head. His feet were bound to the canopy posts. His back shone from oil and sweat. He was stripped to the waist.

Asia, magnificent, stood straddle-legged over him. As Mimi stared in fascinated horror, Bothio flinched from the lash which rained down upon his back. The muscles of his shoulders heaved and rippled like the currents of a stream as he fought against the pain. His face was turned toward Mimi but his eyes were closed.

Then she heard a muttered exclamation. Asia, her magnificent body bending and twisting first this way and then that, with sweat streaming down her every curve and forming rivulets of silver around her full breasts, raised the strap and murmured a half-articulate threat.

"So you would cheat on me, would you?" she screamed. And the furious stroke whipped down again.

The oddest part of the scene to Mimi was that Bothio did not seem to really mind the raging punishment. She could not tear herself away even though she fully realized that it was dangerous to be discovered by either of them in this intimate and private scene.

She closed her eyes and leaned against the door frame, weak and spent. She was sure she was going to faint. Then, just before blackness descended, she felt strong hands grasp her and pull her quickly away.

When she came to, Griff was bending over her. She was lying on a soft sofa in the most beautiful room she had ever seen. A little to one side, standing and watching her with satirical concern and a strange half-smile at the corners of his mouth, was Bothio. Even as she stared at him, Asia sauntered into view.

"Well, what happened to you?" she demanded. "We thought you were never coming out of that one!"

Mimi struggled to sit up. "I'm sorry. I—I must have fainted. I'm a little tired. The last show was really something."

"It must have been," Asia answered shortly. "Well, if you can stand on your feet, let's eat. I'm starved." She led the way to a circular table set in the center of the room.

It's no wonder you are hungry, Mimi thought. After that work-out. Or was it all a dream? She could hardly believe it had really happened. She watched Asia, studied her sinuous, cat-like grace, and she wondered and pondered.

A large mahogany serving table gleamed with shining silver, clear crystal and translucent dinnerware. There were dishes of all kinds—meat and fowl, vegetables and sauces. Champagne was being chilled on a low table near by. Mimi wondered if all the food was for just the four of them. If so, Nick Bothio really lived it up.

"Is all this food for us—just us?" she asked in a voice that sounded small and thin to her ears. Bothio sauntered over to her until he was so close that she could see the deep, inner blackness of his eyes. She shivered.

"Is there someone you would like to invite? Any friend of yours—the right kind, of course—would be a friend of mine." He gave her a piercing look. "That is, if you say so."

Mimi heard a loud pop beside her and turned, startled. Silky was pouring bubbling wine into glasses. Champagne. With his mincing steps, he brought the tray of glasses filled with the golden liquid over to her. As she took one and raised it to her lips, her eyes met his and saw the blue-beaded lashes tremble against the powdered cheeks and the carmined lips curve into a knowing smile. She turned from him and Bothio and crossed the room.

I wonder who caught me just before I fainted, Mimi asked herself. She had had no time to ask Griff if he had been the one. And there was something about Silky...

She watched him as he moved from guest to guest, serving the wine. She had to get to Griff to find out. But Bothio was talking to him.

She gazed uncertainly about her. The room was decorated in several shades of green and silver. The furniture was obviously custom-made, and the walls were covered with a shimmering silk damask in a pattern that she could not quite make out. Something about it looked familiar and she walked closer to the wall to examine it. After a moment of study, her face flamed. She had seen pictures like these when she was in school. Greek myths, the teacher had said, explaining the origins of the art.

Other guests arrived and Bothio led them to the center table. There were four other couples. One of the men was tall and lanky and blond and reminded Mimi of Philip Thornton. She began thinking of the promise she and Griff had made to play for the Thorntons at their birthday party the coming weekend.

The lanky blond, whose name was Sam Watkins, stared at her and Mimi found he was to sit on her left at supper. The others were already seated at the table and calling to her. Bothio's eyes were cynical as Griff pulled out her chair.

"I see you don't appreciate exotic art, Mimi," he drawled.

"Whatic art?" Mimi questioned stupidly.

"Strange art—but symbolizing the very stuff of which life is made." He spoke softly but there was a sharp timbre to his voice that Mimi felt and found disturbing.

Her wide-eyed stare became more pronounced. "I don't know anything about symbols. Sex is sex! What else?" Her shrug was eloquent.

Bothio gave her a keen look. "Yes. That's what I like about you. You are so fundamental, Mimi. Everything is exactly what it is supposed to be, isn't it?"

She still looked vacant. "What else?" She was beginning to be bored by his strange talk. "I don't understand. I was born. I am here. I love Griff. I'll die some day. That's all there is to life."

"Not quite," Bothio murmured. "But I understand you perfectly." He pulled at his shirt cuffs. His face was pale. "I wish my life was that simple. I would undo a lot of things I've done." A stem expression crossed his face. "I was born. I am here. I love everybody—and nobody." He turned to her with the familiar, quizzical smile. "You know, a psychologist once told a judge that I was incapable of love. Imagine! Why, Bothio loves everybody. But there is more to it than just that."

"Did you always want to be such a big-shot, Nicky?" Asia asked, slurring her accent.

"Say that I *had* to be a big-shot," he answered shortly.

"So you just happened to be what you are," Mimi said as she helped herself to something fragrant from a dish that Silky was holding for her.

"Perhaps. But I doubt it. The youngest in a large family, I was always alone, always left out. So I promised myself that when I grew up I would be the top guy, the big-shot. So here I am and here we are."

"Well, I never wanted to be a singer," said Mimi. "I just wanted to get the hell out of a home where my Pa was always scrapping with my Ma and there was never enough to eat."

"I guess we all have something we're running away from, eh, Griff?" Bothio turned to the musician, who had not spoken. "What are you running away from?"

Griff puckered his lips as if in deep thought but before he could answer—

"Sex, most likely," Asia said. Griff flushed scarlet, a flush which left his face paler than Mimi had ever seen it.

"Well!" Bothio said. "Could it be that Asia hit home, boy? Don't worry. We won't pry into your secrets. Bothio always protects his friends. Besides, who knows what's normal and what isn't?"

Griff tried to pull himself together, forcing a jovial tone. "There's no secret. No siree. I just wanted to play my stick and my folks had other ideas. So I picked up my stick one day and blew—literally and figuratively speaking. I've been blowing ever since."

"And you sure make sweet music," Asia's husky contralto broke in. Griff looked at her and smiled. Asia did not take her green eyes away. Mimi saw the pupils dilate and the woman's nostrils quiver.

"The truth is that everybody has some bogey he doesn't want to face," Bothio went on softly. Mimi thought his tone was sinister. "Everybody lives off somebody else. So what's the difference? We're all parasites anyhow," he stated flatly.

Asia still smiled and rolled her big eyes at Griff while Mimi did a slow burn. If she could only get that Asia alone, what she wouldn't do to her. At that moment she even hated Griff.

She turned blazing eyes toward Asia only to be met by Bothio's knowing stare. He always seemed to know everything that was going on. Impulsively she smiled back.

"You live such an exciting life that I wonder how you can tolerate those of us who aren't so exciting," she ventured.

"You think my life is exciting?" His glance was sardonic.

"Well, it seems to be. Running this club and all."

"Would you like to live an exciting life, too? I should imagine that singing with the band is exciting—in its way."

Sensing the banter in his voice, she knew he was teasing her. "It has its moments. But it's pretty routine after a while. It looks much more glamorous than it really is," she admitted candidly.

"Would you do something different if you had the chance?" he persisted, an odd note coming into his voice. "Something much more dangerous and exciting, too?"

"I don't know. I've never done anything but sing," she answered uncertainly. How this man frightened her!

"Who knows? You might be called on to try your hand at other things—some time."

She turned to Griff. He was fiddling with a crumb on the table and she wondered if he had been listening to her conversation with Bothio. Surely he would not be jealous.

Then Asia's contralto laughter rang out. "Did you hear that, Nick? Griff is going to write something extra special for me—his own music, a real Griff Stamm arrangement, no less!"

"That's what I expected him to do, doll," Bothio answered dryly.

"I know what's let's do now!" Asia exclaimed suddenly, with high gaiety. "Let's go try out Griff's ideas for my number."

Griff stared at her. "You kiddin'? I haven't even had time to think about the act yet."

"Oh, well, you'll think as we go along. At least you can see me dance."

"You can talk to Griff all you want about the number," Bothio answered, "but no dancing this morning."

Asia jumped up from the table, her red hair waving wildly. She grabbed Griff's hand. "Let's go on stage and talk about the spotlights then. You know you have to experiment with me—on account of my hair and my fair skin. I look positively greenish if the lights aren't right." Griff allowed himself to be dragged along like a lamb to the sacrificial altar.

After they left, Bothio turned to Mimi. "It looks as if you will have to entertain me." His crooked smile played about the corners of his mouth.

Mimi looked around. "Where are the others?" she inquired.

"Oh, they have gone in search of other entertainment." He waved his hand languorously.

"I don't know how to entertain anyone like you," Mimi answered, scared.

"It isn't hard," he told her. "I'm not a difficult man—when you get to know me. But don't ever try crossing me. Then I'm not nice."

The hard look flickered across his face again. She had heard such sinister stories of this man that she could not relax in his presence.

At length he touched her elbow. "Well, before I make a complete fool of myself, what say we go look up Asia and Griff, eh?" He led the way and soon they were in the Place. From time to time Mimi heard voices and laughter behind the closed doors they passed. But Bothio had become grim and distant. She could hardly keep up with his vigorous stride.

They came at last to a room that was completely dark except for the bright spotlight pinpointing Asia on stage as she whirled in a wild uninhibited dance to Griff's improvised accompaniment.

Mimi, entranced, watched Asia. Her own body was strictly Grade A, but Asia's body was incomparable. Her breasts were full and firm though not as large as Mimi's voluptuous ones. Her slim waist curved to flat slender hips, almost boyish, and her legs were long and beautiful.

But it was the expression on the dancer's face that was hypnotic. It was pure barbaric wildness and savagery. She looked like a jungle animal thrusting and whirling, moved by an inner and wholly irresistible force. Her green eyes were distended, her full red lips parted. The mass of heavy, orange-colored hair swung and danced about the white alabaster throat as if to throttle it. Escaping tendrils caressed the flushed, moist skin of her face.

Asia spun in rhythm to the rapid tempo of Griff's music. Faster and faster she moved until Mimi thought she too would be caught up in the mad spinning of the music and the dance. Then suddenly the music died. Asia fell in a white heap on the stage. But like a deer in the forest, she was up in an instant and running to Bothio.

Taking his face in both her hands, she bent her head to his neck. Bothio cried out. And then Asia was gone. Bothio was wiping his neck with a spotless handkerchief. As his dark, brooding eyes met Mimi's, she saw bright crimson blood on the virgin whiteness of the cloth.

FOUR

FOREST GREEN is one of the last remaining large estates on Long Island's North Shore. That it has endured through several generations, intact and still in its original form and contour, is due to the canniness of the original Thornton forebears. Those wily whaling men made sure that a hard will would hold the estate firm. The ensuing generations helped by holding true to the Thornton ideal.

While all around it the large estates and old parcels of land are giving may to the mad push of space-hungry urbanites suddenly discovering the pleasures of suburban living, Forest Green remains aloof, untouchable and imperishable.

The manse, or Big House, as it is called, is located on a high bluff overlooking the tiny, but well-kept harbor of of Quonchoq Yacht Club. And the Quonchoq Yacht Club is owned by Philip Thornton. There isn't much within twenty miles of the area surrounding Forest Green that isn't Thornton-owned.

The Big House is occupied now by Philip Thornton, who had the misfortune to be an only child, and his wife, Leyra. Besides many predatory but distant relatives, there are no heirs to the Thornton millions but Philip.

Nestling snugly on the rise overlooking Quonchoq Bay, the house has a lovely view of blue-green waters below. The red and white striped awnings of the Yacht Club wink back cheerily and the Thornton's forty-foot yacht, *Invincible,* lies serenely rocking in the lapping waters of the harbor.

The house itself is huge, white and sprawling. Each generation of Thorntons has added something to the building so that it is now an architectural hodge-podge, impressive, warm yet strangely aloof. The interior of the manse follows the same general pattern of mixed styles and periods, so that a Chippendale chair faces a Duncan Phyfe, but this mixing of periods in no way affects the graciousness and warmth of the easy Thornton way of life.

One enters Forest Green by passing under a high, curlicued wrought iron gate over which large letters state simply, "WELCOME TO FOREST GREEN." This should not be taken seriously. Admission to the estate is selective, difficult to obtain, and visitors are carefully screened. To make sure of this, a gatekeeper is always on guard in a tiny cubby just inside the gate.

Forest Green has been many things to its many occupants. But to Philip and Leyra it is a haven where they can escape the conventional for a life of their own making.

Philip's childhood and youth were typical of his class and wealth. Later, college and a law degree from Harvard prepared him for his duties as the sole Thornton heir. He had always been quiet and studious—dull to some—so he surprised no one when he settled down to work with purposefulness. It was no surprise either when his engagement was announced to Leyra Winthrop, a childhood friend, the only daughter of a North Shore family almost as old and rich as his.

The Winthrops and Thorntons knew each other well. Leyra and Philip attended the same dancing classes, went boating together in the Sound and grew to adulthood amicably and easily together. She had been the only one of all the children who knew how to handle the shy boy.

It did not occur to either to think of the other as a possible marriage partner until the night before Philip was to sail for Europe with the Air Force to do his share of defending his country and only incidentally protect the Thornton and Winthrop interests.

As they recalled later, it was Leyra who proposed to Philip as he stood in the garden, toying with his Air Force cap awkwardly. He had really come to say goodbye. But to Leyra the sight of tall and slender Philip, in the brand-new uniform, or perhaps the sight of the scrambled eggs insignia on his uniform, had proved too much.

In a burst of warm emotion, she had clasped her arms about the startled young man's neck and burst into tears, moaning over and over that she just knew she'd never see him again. Philip was, at first, too dumbstruck to do anything but stand, gawking stupidly. But the warmth of Leyra's small, rounded body, shaking uncontrollably against him, penetrated his consciousness and he realized with a shock that Leyra had grown up.

He fumbled clumsily and patted her shaking shoulders as the fragrance from her crisp curls tantalized him. Somehow, he never knew exactly how, his lips were against hers and he was being swept away on the most intoxicating journey of his life. Since this was his first really serious kiss, he needed a retake to fully appreciate it.

Before they left the garden, they were engaged. It was again Leyra who brought it about. Very simply she had said, "Oh, Philip, I'll wait for you. I'll wait for you to come back. I'll never love anyone but you."

"Gosh, Leyra! Oh, Gosh!" was all that Philip could manage.

So Leyra waited and Philip returned two years, nine months and eighteen days later. They married, and to all concerned it seemed a good match. Two charming young people had found and loved each other. Two old families could now keep the wealth and status quo. Two sets of parents, or four, including the divorced step-parents, breathed with relief. The young couple settled down in Forest Green to get to know each other and to begin to produce the little Thorntons who were badly needed.

Like the rest of their set, Philip and Leyra rode, sailed and danced at the Forest Green Country Club, which belonged to

Leyra, or partied at the Quochonq Yacht Club, which belonged to Philip. As a child, Leyra had given evidence of becoming an outstanding equestrienne. Philip's sport remained sailing. As "young marrieds," they settled down to their special bents with vigor and enthusiasm.

Leyra attended all the horsey events, rode and won and gallantly gave her winnings to the various charities favored by her set that season. Philip was always in the cheering section to see her ride home. Never demonstrative, the shiny gleam in his blue eyes and the glad smile were the only demonstrations of his joy.

Philip knew heaven when Leyra coyly told him one night that she was about to have their first child. After that he worried about her constantly. He tried to get her to give up riding until after the baby was born. But Leyra waved away his fears. "Oh, silly! You don't have to worry for months yet. I have plenty of time!"

Finally, seeing how her riding upset him, she promised to make her last jump at the special meet of the season—her last jump, that is, until after the birth of the precious heir.

The day of the meet started off well for Philip. He had awakened first. He had laid very still on the double bed he insisted upon, listening to Leyra's even breathing. The morning sun shone through the open windows and through the cottage curtains to form fancy lattice patterns on the yellow carpet.

Yielding to a strong rare urge, Philip had pulled the sleeping form of his wife to him and held her very close. Still asleep, Leyra snuggled to him. He could not understand his strange urge. Leyra had always been the initiator of the love play between them. Now, throughout his being he had felt an overwhelming joy and protective feeling for her.

Later he was to vividly remember that morning and the strange sensation. The meet drew a large crowd. The air was cold and crisp. Excitement churned like electricity as the riders lined up at the post. Philip, astride his own mount on the sidelines, heard the cry, "They're off!" and the roar of the crowd.

He strained to follow Leyra's course but the race was a mad blur of charging horses' legs. Then they were at the first hurdle. It was a short race, with only a few jumps, but it had been made more difficult because of this brevity. Leyra made her first jump clean and in good time. She was well ahead in points. Philip turned his head for a moment.

Then he heard the cry of "She's spilled!" He turned back quickly. Leyra had fallen! He raced his mount. When he reached her, she was already in the ambulance. He was certain that she had lost their child. What he did not know then was that she would never walk again. Or that she could never have another child.

Some people can relate to other human beings easily and readily at first meeting by making them feel at ease, as if they were old friends. Leyra was such a person. Not so with Philip. Perhaps the secret of their successful marriage was this fact— the fact that they balanced each other. Philip, retiring and with-drawn, had come to depend on Leyra's initiative and leadership in social matters. In their physical life also, initiative had come from her.

Psychologists hold that a truly happy sex relationship exists only when both parties take turns in leading and initiating the sex play. In Philip's case, however, Leyra's sexual aggressiveness caused him no discomfort, nor did it affect his male ego in any way. He was normal and knew it. But he derived great satisfac-tion from knowing that Leyra wanted him and always made the first move.

When the shock of the accident had died away and the pro-cess of changing doctors and trying new ones, always hoping for a favorable prognosis, had become routine, both Philip and Leyra had come to accept the fact that she would never walk again. And that, far worse, their sex life together was changed, for Leyra was paralyzed from her waist down.

By the time Leyra returned home from the hospital, all the verdicts of her life-long invalidism were spoken and she and Philip had both come to accept it. Philip was happy just to have her near him again. But to the practical Leyra, another problem became immediately apparent.

One day as Philip was adjusting the blanket about her inert legs, a sudden burst of feeling overcame him and he sank to his knees beside her, burying his blond head in her lap.

"Oh, Leyra, honey!" he cried brokenly.

Leyra stroked his hair gently and her usually tender face became even more soft and radiant. "Philip, what are you going to do now, dearest?" she asked softly.

He raised his head and stared at her vacantly. "Do darling? I don't understand."

Leyra blushed and a film of confusion clouded the directness of her gaze.

"I mean, dear, marital duties are beyond me. And you are a normal man. What will become of us? Of you? Of our marriage?" She hid her face with her hand and a low, poignant cry burst from her. He crushed her shaking shoulders to him and murmured against her wet cheek.

"I want no one but you, darling. I shall never want anyone but you. You know I couldn't," he repeated hoarsely.

That night, as he lifted her out of her chair to put her in bed, he sensed a new excitement emanating from her.

"Darling, don't cover me up. Let's not get under the covers just yet," she whispered tremulously.

"All right, dear," he mumbled, getting in bed beside her and nuzzling her warm shoulder. His lips worried her slender throat. Never had he wanted her more. He was a seething mass, a cauldron of boiling desires. He moaned softly and buried his face in her hair. He felt her moving away from him. Her hands were traveling over his body, making gentle, gliding motions. He could feel the light touches at his chest and on his thighs.

Her lips were against the flatness of his stomach. Her warm breath excited him and his skin pebbled along his thighs. Her face was lost in his body. He stiffened involuntarily, his taut body arched.

"No!" he cried, choked. "No, darling!"

But she only murmured inarticulate sounds and phrases he did not comprehend. He was transported into another world made of dream stuff, floating and sailing on soft clouds. He clung to her hands. Never before had their intimate moments been so beautiful and full of tenderness. Leyra's warmth and generosity, her desire to give him full happiness, overwhelmed him.

Afterwards, they lay quietly, her head resting on his shoulder, her body lax against his. He felt a deep humility and unworthiness. He wanted to purge himself of all his aches and yearnings but words failed him. He wanted to tell her that the part of him that he had given her would always be hers. He hopped she knew it even if he could not express it to her.

Day after day he saw her concern for him growing, gaining importance. He tried to reassurer her. He wanted no one but her and nothing other than what they shared. But she was not to be convinced. It was as if now his happiness was the only object of her life.

"I know I can't fill the role of a wife to you in the normal sense—" She stopped and looked down in confusion. "So I think you ought to do something about it," she finished lamely.

He looked at her foolishly. "Do something about it?" he asked. "What? What are you talking about, Leyra?"

A rosy flush tinted her face. "I mean that I think you ought to look outside of our marriage for—for—for what you can't get from me, darling. I won't mind, really. I'd like you to. You see, I hate knowing that you deprive yourself because I am this way. I feel so guilty."

He stroked her velvet cheek. "Now, look here, wife of mine," he told her huskily. "I love you. You and you alone. You are being deprived more than I and that kills me more than anything else. So we'll have no more of this kind of talk!"

But there had been more talk. Much more. Seeing that she had become obsessed with the matter, he agreed half-heartedly, just to placate her, and promised jokingly to report back to her how things went with his extra-marital adventures. The relief that registered on her heart-shaped face astonished him. So she really had been serious about the mad idea.

One night he got to the train station too late to get the five-fifteen to the Island. He had forty-five minutes to kill before getting the next express. He headed for the nearby bar to wait.

The bar was crowded, as usual at this hour, with men like himself, waiting for trains. He ordered a Scotch and soda and sipped at the drink absently. A high, musically feminine voice spoke beside him in a marked Southern accent.

"I declar' ah don't know how these trains run aroun' heah! Ah'm alus missin' 'em."

Philip turned to gaze into a soft pair of dark eyes. The girl was standing beside him, a petite creature. She smiled winsomely.

"Are you stuck, too—without a train, ah mean? Ah just missed mine."

Philip smiled and nodded sympathetically. "I missed mine all right," he admitted. "I was late this time but for once the train was not."

She laughed merrily and Philip made more room for her beside him. After they finished their drinks, they found seats at a corner table and Liza, "jes' plain ole Liza. That's all. It's not even a nickname," told him about herself, chattering away as if he were an old friend of the family's whom she had just bumped into.

She had recently come up from Nashville, she told him, and was working as a model. She was going to spend the weekend with friends on the Island, "if ah ever get on that train." And it happened that she didn't get on that train that night because she and Philip ended up in her apartment which she shared with an airline stewardess girl friend who, fortunately for them, was away on a flight.

Something about Liza, other than her size, reminded Philip of Leyra. Her body was boyish and slight. She looked like someone's younger brother. Petite and slim, yet rounded, brown and boyish, she was like an eager puppy never keeping still long, always yapping, alive and eager to please.

Philip sat back in a deep chair, drink in hand, and enjoyed her. Her brown eyes lit up and sparkled merrily as she enjoyed her own jokes and laughed at herself.

"Well, you know, it's the funniest thing. There Ah was, a little girl like me, sitting on this sofa next to this great big galoot who was supposed to hug me. An' the photographer standing by waitin' for the clinch—Well! You'd nevah guess what happen! This bear of a man hugs me and the photographer man lets out a shout. He couldn't even *see* me. Ah was completely swallowed *up!* So—"

She went off into a peal of ringing laughter and disappeared, her small buttocks rolling enticingly. She returned wearing a shortie nightgown that made her look even smaller.

The sap rose in Philip. She came over to him and sat on the arm of his chair and tousled his hair.

"Ah just love blond men," Liza whispered huskily, snuggling to him. He clasped her to him but she disengaged herself and gave an embarrassed laugh. "You know, we haven't talked about the business end of this yet, honey," she said. "It'll cost you. Fifty dollars, to be exact."

He looked at her stupidly. "Oh. Of course!" and he pulled out his wallet and laid the money on the nearby table.

"Now aren't you the good sport, honey? How nice!" She picked up the money and disappeared into the bedroom. When she returned, she took his arm and led him to the bed. He began to sense an undercurrent of impersonality about her manner. This was only a business with her. He hesitated at the door, his hands in his pockets.

Liza lay on the bed, stretched out. "C'mon, honey. You might as well start collectin' and get your money's worth."

A weakness began to steal over Philip. He walked inside the room and undressed slowly. Then he stretched out on the bed beside Liza. He made no move to touch her. She turned to him and began caressing his body. He sensed a detached haste about her movements now.

He could not get aroused. Her actions became fevered but they aroused no emotion in him. He got up, dressed and walked to the station and took the first train home.

Leyra was reading in bed when he got in. He sat on the side of the bed and took her tiny hand in his. Then without shame or fear, knowing she would understand, he told her. When he finished, he rested his head on her lap. He felt debased and inadequate.

"My poor, dear Philip. It's all my fault but I so want you to be happy—fully happy, I mean."

He raised his head. "I know. But you know what I think it is? I can't react normally with anyone else but you. I don't suppose you've guessed. Maybe you have at that, but you've been the only woman in my life, Leyra. I don't—I don't think I could ever have anyone else."

"Darling! I love that. But now, with me in this state—something has to be done!"

"Nothing can be done, need be done. So we might as well enjoy each other as we have been doing."

He spoke with finality. He got up and began undressing and got in bed beside her. Deep wells inside him were stirring. This was his life, his beloved, the only woman for him. He wanted nothing more.

Her fingers were playing on his body lightly, like a million tiny, flitting butterflies. Her lips caressed his face, his eyelids. Then they were on his mouth. He felt her warm breath in a quick gasp. Then her mouth was on his body. Her hands grasped the muscles of his thighs. The tension exploded into a thousand vari-colored sparks. He was floating and drifting on soft clouds which enveloped him gently. He was at peace.

The next afternoon he and Leyra were sunning themselves on the boat deck. "You know what I think is the matter with you, darling?"

"What?" he asked.

"I think you need to have me near when you make love to someone else. You know, to give you the feeling that I am sharing in the experience with you. Perhaps I could hold your hand or something. ..."

She stopped in confusion as he stared at her, shocked. After a moment he answered more sharply than he intended. "I don't want to try any more," he said gruffly.

"I thing you ought to," she replied firmly, "just to prove to yourself that you can."

His eyes focused on her face. "With whom?"

But Leyra, feeling that she had won the first round, decided not to press further. "Oh, someone will turn up," she said lightly, smiling.

The matter rested there and might have remained unchanged but for the course of circumstances. One day Philip's lawyers brought up the question of his inheritance. Leyra's accident and the subsequent improbability of her ever having a child raised questions. Who would inherit the vast Thornton holdings? Had Philip been thinking of these matters?

He was annoyed and irritated. These were not things he wanted to give much thought to. He and Leyra had worked out a pattern of living for themselves and they were both content. It mattered little to him who inherited the Thornton millions. He had no intention of discussing this with Leyra, knowing just what she would suggest. And he so informed the wise and learned attorneys.

But the matter did not end there. Somehow it got to Leyra and she was waiting for him when he got home one day, determined to find a solution to the problem. It was their custom to have coffee and brandy in the library after dinner.

"I saw the doctor again today," she told him. "It seems that the chances of my ever having a child are almost non-existent. If I were even to conceive—by some miracle—I couldn't carry it full term," she said softly. "So we have to think of something—else."

"All right, what?" Philip asked, not expecting her to come up with anything constructive.

"Well, I—I guess we could adopt a child."

"Sorry. I thought of that. The lawyers nixed that fast. They said relatives of the adoptive child might crop up and present complications—or some of my distant relatives might object on the blood line basis. I am afraid that's out!"

Leyra was silent for a moment. "Wel-l-l, you could have a child—through a—a—test tube mother—or something."

Philip was astonished. "Really, Leyra. Now I guess that's the limit!"

"The mother doesn't have to know who you are. And we can adopt the child later—under a legal contract and everything."

"I am afraid that won't do either. You can see that, darling." Philip closed his eyes and stretched. "Better give up the idea. But it is true that a natural child would have legal claim before any other heirs."

A few day later Leyra and he were alone. He felt her eyes on him speculatively. "No-o-o. I guess you wouldn't anyhow. But I feel it could work."

"What could work?" he asked, piqued by her mysterious air.

But Leyra, womanlike, skirted the question by raising another. "Don't you think it's time you tried to prove your prowess again?"

He thought a moment. "You seem to be more anxious about this thing than I am," he said, smiling.

"Yes. I think it's because I feel so guilty and inadequate."

He walked over to her chair and kissed her lightly on the forehead. "Well, just forget it."

Yet fate has a way of stepping in and altering plans. It was the day following this conversation when, coming back from a nearby town on a visit to one of his classmates, he came face-to-face with his destiny. Driving along the highway, his car developed brake trouble, then a flat. Up ahead was a blinking neon sign. Hoping to find a telephone to call a garage, he walked up the road and stepped into the Paradise Club.

Since he was tired from his walk and irritable and would surely miss his dinner, he decided to have a snack. While he was waiting to be served, a singer, lush and provocative, came on stage.

Philip stared, open-mouthed. She was the loveliest thing he had ever seen in his life. Tiny but rounded in the right places, with ebony curls swirling about her oval face in which enormous violet eyes flamed and sparkled, she was like a blow in the chest to Philip.

He listened to her singing, spellbound. And for the first time since marrying Leyra, he knew that he had seen another girl whom he could truly possess. His hands were shaking. Fine sweat broke out on his lips and temples. He called the waiter over and made inquiries about her. But he made no effort to speak to her or to get to know her.

As the days passed, he found that he could not forget her, and impulsively he described the girl to Leyra.

Leyra was quick to pounce on the opportunity and she worked swiftly and cleverly, making contacts and plans with all the know-how of a polished diplomat—much to Philip's amazement and consternation.

Now Mimi and Griff were to entertain at his birthday party. This would give him the opportunity to observe Mimi closely, to see if she would really be a fitting partner for the mad idea Leyra had in mind. After all, a Thornton heir had to meet some specifications, he mused. But he found that he was looking forward to the adventure for other reasons—reasons purely of his own.

FIVE

M IMI gazed at the passing countryside without interest. She and Griff were being driven to the Thornton estate in the Thornton's limousine. Two members of the band and their instruments were following behind in the band's station wagon.

Mimi was one of those rare people whom money could not touch. To her elemental nature, the only things that mattered were the things she needed from day to day. And she had in her tiny, curvaceous body all she had ever required to get what she wanted out of life. Now that she had Griff with her, her one unfulfilled ambition was marriage.

Griff's attitude was altogether different. To him, wealth meant ease and the freedom to compose and arrange the kind of music that took the time and leisure to create. Money meant an end to one-night stands and cheap lodgings on the road and the uncertainty of tours and the end to coping with temperamental would-be musicians, most of whom had to be taught music and shown how to play their instruments.

He was looking forward to this weekend at the Thorntons. He hoped to solidify the proposition they had made to Mimi. He and Mimi were a strange twosome, he knew—with a rare musical compatability that enabled them to do beautiful, exciting, musical things together. He knew, too, that he was a naturally talented musician. More than anything he wanted to develop and explore the music that lay deep within him.

Music was his whole life. The only thing he had ever really wanted was to become the best clarinet player possible. From his teens on, he knew he was going to be big time. He felt it all through him.

But Mimi brought out something no one else had ever evoked. She mattered to him, yes. He knew she loved him but somehow, something, he didn't know what, kept him from fully loving her. This puzzled him and lately he was beginning to wonder and sulk and the new feelings were making him morose.

He never showed it. Only when he was alone did he let himself go. Often he desired Mimi with a hunger and passion so great that they overpowered him. He would hold her in his arms and thrill to the sweet softness of her provocative and yielding body pressing warm against him, only to feel all emotion die suddenly at the crest of their love-making.

And then recently he noticed that when he was with Bothio he was unusually flustered and ill at ease. This disturbed him. He tried not to think about it, for thinking was upsetting and that was one thing he couldn't afford. Too much depended on him. He had seen too many guys go by the board when the pressures got too great and take to the bottle or to the white stuff.

So perhaps what he needed was to get away from pressures, and this Thornton deal might do it. This might be the pass-key to ease and peace of mind for both himself and Mimi.

As they drove up the wide driveway to the veranda, he knew he had reached a turning point in his life. From here on, it was going to be either the big time for him or the end. This was to be his chance. He intended to do all he could to bring it off.

Of the members of the band, he had brought only Tubby Marshall and Chink Jones. Tubby was a big slob of a man but he was terrific on the eighty-eight and could beat a mean rhythm. Besides, he doubled on the string bass. The only trouble with Tubby was that he used the stuff. A real main-liner. His fat moon face always had a vacant look and his mouth was always open, drooling after something vague in his ever-foggy dreams.

The other man, Chink Jones, blew a hot trombone and doubled on the skins. The two men were good. With them and Mimi,
Griff knew he could hold any crowd, even the fast-stepping, fast-
living Thornton group. He intended to give them a lot for the
money. It would pay off later—on the other deal.

As the car and wagon stopped and they all piled out and
stretched their legs, he heard Tubby whine.

"Man, I've gotta have a fix. I thought this hearse would never
get here!"

Griff frowned. He didn't want any mix-ups. "Now look,
Tubby! I don't want any crosses, hear, man? Keep it level, on an
even beat, man."

Tubby's whine became more pronounced. "I'm not gonna
do nuthin'. I just gotta pop, man. I just gotta. That's all. I'll be
straight in no time."

Ordinarily Griff never used a man if he knew he was on the
stuff. He would be too much trouble and undependable. But
Tubby was a first-rate musician and so far had been no trouble.
And Griff hadn't known he was a main-liner until it was too late.
He was still frowning as he heard Leyra's soft voice at the door
where she and Philip waited to greet them.

Mimi had never been inside such a big house before. She was
sure she would lose her way if she had to live in it. And she was
dying a slow death just at the idea of spending the weekend there.

"The house is old but really charming and I love it," Leyra was
saying sweetly. "We have private guest cabins on the grounds so
you can take your pick—the Big House or a cabin all your own."

"Well-l-l, I think I'll start off tonight in the Big House and
see what happens tomorrow," Mimi replied cautiously.

Leyra laughed merrily. "All right then! You'll be comfortable
enough. You'll see. Then I'll be near and I'm glad because we can
see each other more often here than if you were in a guest house,"
she added warmly. "The party tomorrow night is to be a costume
affair. You can have your pick of the costumes in the sewing

room. I bet you'll look awfully cute in whatever you choose. You are *much* too beautiful." She eyed Mimi openly without a trace of malice or envy. "I wouldn't blame Philip for wanting you madly," she said casually. "Oh! One thing more. My friends are pretty wild sometimes at our parties. You know, life is pretty dull for most of them—too much money and not enough to do—so don't be upset by anything odd you might see. They won't be meaning any harm, really. I just thought I'd prepare you. You look so young and cuddly."

Mimi thought she detected an odd undercurrent in Leyra's voice and wondered about it.

Leyra left and Mimi stepped through the tall French doors to the broad balcony that ran the length of the house. The white roofs of the guest cottages peeped through the trees a little distance away. A few short steps from the house and on her left the water in the large swimming pool glistened like polished glass. The scent of flowering shrubs came to her. April was in its full array. The luxurious beauty and charm of Forest Green was reaching her.

The party promised to be very exciting. Signs of festivity were everywhere. Gay-colored Japanese lanterns hung from the ceilings in the patios and on the shrubbery surrounding the swimming pool. Strings of brilliant electric light bulbs were strung across the lawn and in the branches of the trees bordering the Big House and the cottages fringing it.

Mimi thought of Leyra and Philip and the madness of their proposition. She didn't mind having a child, she told herself. It was only that she wanted a child of Griff's—and he would have none of that idea. Just think! She had to have a child for an absolutely strange man before Griff would allow her to have one for him.

She walked along the veranda and suddenly she saw the bay below. A boat was lying at anchor, white and trim. She wondered if she would be spending part of the weekend on it. She felt a thrill at the thought for the sea had always been one of her prime passions. Sunlight flicked changing patterns on the water. It would be so nice if she and Griff had a boat of their own to escape to. Perhaps this deal might work out well after all.

In the Big House was a ballroom running its entire length. At one time this had been the original Captain's apartment. The old nautical decorations remained on the walls and the dark mahogany beams still gleamed in the flickering light. The highly polished hardwood floor shone black and the bright decorations made a lively contrast against it.

Guests had been arriving for hours. People were constantly coming and going through the multitude of doors. Mimi finally stopped trying to remember faces. The band was mounted on a platform at one end of the ballroom. The old grand piano had retained a surprisingly good tone.

Tubby had got his fix and was flying as he put it "higher than a Georgia pine." Now he was prodding Griff. "Let's go, man. Let's go!"

Mimi had rummaged through dozens of costumes and decided on a bright scarlet fluffy thing with red tights that covered her from neck to toes. The skin-fitting costume showed off every curve and line of her slim body. Over the tights she slipped the red tuttu skirt. Now she looked like a ballerina. She whirled before the mirror. The skirt fluffed and dipped as she moved. Her violet eyes were so ablaze with excitement that they looked almost black. Her dark curls glistened in contrast to the paleness of her creamy skin. She thrilled with self-admiration. She was beautiful!

She started down the stairs on dancing feet. Her red and white ballet slippers made no sound. She heard Tubby improvising at the piano. Then Griff's clarinet came up from under with fast riffs and curlicues in a variation on Tubby's theme.

Her heart pounded with excitement. She knew that something unusual was going to happen to her tonight. She could just feel it.

Clusters of costumed people were standing or sitting on the steps. All wore masks. She hurriedly put hers on, her eyes dancing impishly. She inched her way on down the stairs. As she reached the bottom, someone clasped her tightly by the waist. She stared into the masked face of Mephistopheles. A deep, throbbing male voice spoke in her ear.

"I claim you as my first victim!"

She could feel the strong cords of his arms as they flexed against her body. A thrill shot through her. She searched the face for some feature to be recognized later when the masks were removed at midnight. She could find nothing, and suddenly rough arms pried them apart. A heavy-set, tall man pulled her away from Mephisto.

"Oh, no you don't! You can't claim this delectable queen all for yourself!" He pulled Mimi toward him determinedly. "I am the Ace of Spades!" he thundered. He was dressed in a costume to match hers—minus the tuttu and in colors of black and white.

Then, before she or her companion could protest, Ace of Spades lifted her and slung her over his massive shoulders and elbowed his way into the ballroom. The band had already begun playing. Mimi could tell by the way Tubby was laying it on the ivories that it was going to be one of those terrific nights when each of them sparked one another and they made really good music.

She began to feel the pulse of the music. She wanted to be up on the platform next to Griff, sharing the current, but Ace of Spades had no intention of letting her go. He swung her rapidly around the ballroom floor.

"Boy! Tonight this baby's gonna have himself a ball!" he chortled. "My wife left for Europe two days ago—just in time for this party." He looked down at her from his lofty height. "First time at one of Leyra's parties?" he asked. "I never saw you around here before. I would have recognized that body—mask or no mask!"

Mimi sensed that he meant no harm and was just a hen-pecked husband trying to be a playboy the first chance he got. When they collided with several couples, she took the opportunity to slip away from the wishful Casanova.

She pushed and fought her way to the platform. Chick was whacking away at the skins. He and Tubby were having a ball with the rhythm. Griff had stopped playing at his first pause after seeing her. His face was flushed and his eyes glowed the way they did whenever he played the stick. She felt the excitement that always flared up when they worked together. She and Griff discharged music into each other. They imparted this feeling to the others and blasted it to the audience.

She stepped up to the bandstand and began to sing right in the middle of the number. Griff was dressed as a harlequin, his blue and white diamonds matching his blond hair that glistened like moonlight. He watched her closely. Her eyes were like deep, black wells in the pale, white face. Her hips swayed from side to side in the free, flowing stride that was all hers. She had the detached air so familiar when she was hearing and feeling music deep inside her. Then she was at the mike, matching his gaze. Her taut body, thighs tight and sensuous, moved slightly in time with the music.

He could feel the tension mount within him. He was on fire just as she was. Music and love affected him in the same way. He wanted her with a burning passion. But he knew it was no use. Dear God, why did he always lose it at the last? Why did he always grow cold when he was with her? He cared for her more than he had ever cared for anyone. What was wrong with him? He lifted the long stick to his lips and poured his heart and soul into the music. He knew she would understand. And as if in answer, Mimi sang with him. The song was a pure mating call.

The music became intoxicating. The audience lapped it up and asked for more. Mimi felt that subtle communication that often exists between an audience and a performer when the audience is receptive and the performer is "in the groove."

Time passed and figures paraded before Mimi's eyes in a kaleidoscope of color like shadows in a dream. A wispy blonde Columbine flashed a smile to her and called out while hanging on to the arms of a savage, primitive Indian Chief with an impassive face. She caught a glimpse of Mephisto whirling like a dervish, clasping a golden nymph with fragile wings. Keep the beat, keep it level, stay with it. Keep the beat! Boom! Boom! Ta! Ta! Boom! Boom! Ta! Ta! Music man, play. Oh, Griff! She was on fire. She wanted him. She had to sing to get the tension out of her. Keep the beat! Keep the beat!

Then there came the break. People hung about in groups and clusters, chatting and watching. A deep voice bellowed above the chatter and Mimi recognized it as belonging to the Ace of Spades. He was threading his way through the crowd to the platform. She clung to the microphone.

"Hi, ya, doll! Gonna catch up with you before the night is old!" he promised, staring at her. Then, suddenly grabbing the mike from her, he yelled into it. "We're going to have some entertainment, folks. A different kind from what you've been having up to now. We're going to play some games. Husbands take a long look at your wives—'cause you won't be seeing them again for a while."

He paused for effect. Then, raising his voice again, "The Slave Auction is coming up!" he shouted, "And you know what that means!"

There was a loud cheer from the audience. An electric tension vibrated in the room. Everyone waited expectantly.

"Will all the ladies gather together at this end of the room and prepare to be sold to the highest bidder. Please! Get ready to come up to the platform when your number is called. You will be given numbers—and please, for God's sake, keep your masks on. We don't want anybody to be able to recognize anyone else," he exhorted earnestly.

There was general nervous laughter. Several men began hanging number tags on the women's costumes as they hurriedly grouped near the platform. Griff and his men began to leave the bandstand. Mimi started on her way down but he caught her elbow.

"Hey, doll! You look sorta cute in that outfit. Mind if I stay around a while?" he asked in mock seriousness.

"I was just beginning to feel very neglected," she pouted, hugging his arm close against her side. "I haven't seen you in hours. How is your cottage?"

He waved his hand languidly. "Everything is strictly big time here. See what I mean about taking it cool on Easy Street, baby? This is living!"

She nodded. He led her to the veranda where a cool breeze blew from the bay. Below, the yacht lay bright and serene. Griff was quiet. When he spoke again, his voice was warm with admiration.

"That cruiser is some beauty. I looked her over. She's sure beautiful. Want to go down and look?"

"Griff, you're kidding."

"No, baby. I'm serious. That boat is real crazy. Phillip took me over her. You know, he's a right guy. Real great. Told me I could board her any time I feel like it."

"I would love to go aboard," Mimi said. "Can we go tonight?"

"I don't see why not. They're going to be having some games and stuff like that for a long time. We can sneak away."

"I want to go upstairs for a minute. I'm dripping. Will you wait until I come back?"

"Sure. But don't take too long primping. I'll meet you at by the door."

"All right, I'll be right down." She called back over her should as she hurried away.

She pushed through a clique standing at the door and headed for the stairs leading to the second floor. She glanced back at the ballroom. Several girls were lined up on the platform. The auctioneer, none of than the Ace of Spades, as selling them to the highest bidder. The girl being sold was the tiny blonde with the fairy wings. She stood knee bent, her face coyly downcast.

"What do I get for this adorable blonde fluff?" Ace of Spades bellowed. "What do I get? Remember Leyra's favorite charity needs money."

Several men quickly raised their hands and named fantastic sums of money. Mimi stared, astonished. She could hardly believe that they were bidding real money. She turned to the man standing beside her.

"Is this for real? I mean, are they bidding real money?"

"What, babe? Hey, you should be up there," he exclaimed, raking her lithe form with his eyes.

"Is this for real?" she persisted.

"Oh sure, and everybody pays up, too. This is a regular feature at Leyra's parties—for charity, you know. All in fun." He chuckled. "The best fun is to try not to bid on your own wife."

"Oh!" Mimi was awed. "But how do you know who you are bidding for?"

"That's the best part of it. You don't. Costumes are always a deep, dark secret."

"You mean nobody ever knows who anybody is?"

"That's right. Nobody ever knows afterwards, either."

She turned away, numbed.

"Hey, aren't you going up there?" he called after her.

"No, everybody knows who I am by this time."

She hurried upstairs, repaired her make-up, and put her mask back on. Griff would be waiting for her by the door and he hated to be kept waiting. She hurried back to the front door and dashed around to the side of the house to call Griff from the lawn under the veranda. No use pushing through the crowd again to reach him.

As she turned the corner of the house, a tall, bulky man sprang out of the shrubbery and grabbed her firmly by the arms. She tried to scream, but her breath was swallowed by the coarse material of the man's costume. She was struggling desperately when a pair of gay revelers came upon them. Her unknown assailant begrudgingly released his hold. He gave a low grunt. Mimi took advantage of the distraction and bolted into the green of the shrubs bordering the house.

The shrubbery curved along the side of the pool where prone figures lay closely entwined. Mimi ran headlong, terrified. She could hear the heavy steps of the man pursuing her. Her breath came in short jerks. She increased her speed. Her heart was bursting in her chest.

She ran wildly, pell mell, not knowing where she was heading. Beyond her was light. Without thinking, she ran toward it. She stumbled and landed on all fours. Her pursuer's footsteps came on. She scrambled up and dashed wildly ahead. The lights were only a little way off. With a burst of speed brought on by her terror, she raced on.

Suddenly she stopped short, confused. The grass had ended. She was standing on a pebbled walk. The bay was before her. The boat lay at anchor a few steps away. Without a thought, she followed the runway that led to the lighted haven. She flew down the slim gangplank.

She never stopped to look back to see if her pursuer had followed. There were lights, and lights meant safety. She was so distracted and winded that she failed to see the tall figure in her path. She was running along the narrow deck of the boat when she bumped into him.

"Oh!" she gasped, breathless. "Griff! I am so glad you're here! A man—he chased me all the way down here. I was so frightened. Oh, Griff. I—I—"

She was overcome and incoherent and clung to him. The harlequin held her close. She snuggled up to him, trembling. He led her to a nearby cabin. It was dim and cool inside. The only light came from a shaded lamp hanging on the wall which emitted a dim, cozy haze.

She was led to a bunk. She sank down on the softness, still trembling violently. She could hear him moving about. Then a glass was pressed to her lips. She drank the burning liquor in gulps. Gentle hands began to undress her.

Still shivering, she gave herself up without hesitation. Griff was so kind. He had never undressed her before. They lay close together. He covered her shaking body with his own warm one. She felt his lips in her hair. Then there was the tender pilgrimage—the quest over her ear and eyelids. She felt the warm, seeking kisses on her neck. Her body arched involuntarily toward him, as naturally as a green thing seeks the sun.

Her hunger was young and wild and he responded to it ardently. Never had she known such sweet fulfillment. Life became a whirling cloud that floated high above and changed colors and merged, only to burst like colored balloons and then, at last, to melt together again.

The earth spun and rocked and the clasped figures rocked with it. An agonized cry burst from her. "Oh, Griff! Griff!"

At last she left the still slowly floating clouds and drifted down to earth. She was warm and damp. Moisture clung to her heated body. She was relaxed and at peace. Her flesh was weightless. Turning over on her side, she stretched luxuriously. Her eyes took in the form of the man beside her.

For an awful second she stared. "No-o-o-o-o!" she cried. But it was only a whisper. She covered her face with her hands. "Oh, no!" Cruel sobs wracked her. This man at her side was not Griff, but Philip.

At her cry he sat up instantly. "Please, Mimi! Please don't be angry. I couldn't help myself. You came to me—and I—I thought that you had decided in favor of—"

He was contrite. Mimi forced herself to face him. "I didn't know it was you. You were wearing the same harlequin costume as Griff—and you are the same height and build—and I was so scared and confused that I—" She began to cry again.

He looked crestfallen and whipped. "I am sorry. Truly sorry. I thought you came to me."

He rose from the bunk. His body glistened pale and strong in the dim light. Then he turned to her again. "That's not exactly true. I did have a strange feeling that you weren't sure it was me—but—" he paused and smiled down at her. "It was the most beautiful..." He stopped in confusion.

At his words Mimi stopped crying and stared at him. It *had* been beautiful. The most beautiful she had ever known. Somehow it seemed wrong to spoil it now—to mar the perfection and purity of it, destroying the memory forever. She was not an innocent ingenue after all. It had been an honest mix-up. And it was already done. And, Mimi faced the fact boldly, she didn't want to undo it! Griff had never reached such heights with her. There was always something wanting as he held himself back from completely sharing with her.

She faced Philip and spoke honestly. "It was the most beautiful for me, too," she admitted. "I don't mean to spoil it. Beside, it's done already—and—" a bitter smile turned her lips, "as you say, that is why I am here. It's just that I hadn't really decided yet. But maybe it's just as well."

"Then you are not sorry?" Philip asked her wistfully. "Please, Mimi, don't be sorry. You see," he explained awkwardly, "you see, you are the first one other than Leyra who..." He could not go on.

He was miserable. Her heart softened. She went to him and touched his arm. "No. I'm not sorry. It's done and I think I'd do it over again," she said simply.

He drew her to him slowly. She could feel him straining against her, his muscles beginning to throb again.

"I hope you two don't mind my coming in, but this seems to be the best entrance I've ever made in my life!"

Leyra's voice struck them, wrenching Mimi from Philip cruelly.

"No. Mimi, please! It's all right. Really it is. I am not playing the role of the injured, jealous wife." Her voice was pleasant. Mimi stared at her in amazement. "You see," Leyra went on as she maneuvered her chair into the room, "I love my husband deeply. And because I can't fulfill his love normally, I must look for other means to do so. I am really very happy at the outcome of my little scheme." She smiled. "I had no idea it would work out so well!"

"What little scheme?" Mimi asked.

"Why, having two harlequin costumes, of course. You don't think it was an accident that both Philip and Griff were wearing identical harlequin costumes do you? I had hoped there would be just such a mix-up as this to make things easier." She laughed gaily. "And here we all are. It worked out just fine. Simply fine!"

In spite of her embarrassment, Mimi could not help warming toward Leyra. The woman showed no resentment and Mimi marveled at the depth of a love that could be so self-sacrificing. Suddenly her legs began to give way. She clung to the bunk to keep from falling. The night had been a confusing one.

"Oh, Philip! I think she's going to faint. Shock! Please get her a drink."

Mimi heard Leyra from far away. Then a drink was forced between her lips. It was hot and burning and she began to feel a warmth permeating her. She lay on the bunk again and Leyra held the glass to her lips.

"Philip, please go to the galley and get her something to eat. I bet she's not eaten for hours."

While Philip was gone, Leyra's eyes greedily raked Mimi's lush form. They shone bright and hard. Mimi felt soft fingers like fragile tendrils coursing down her body. The tendrils were clinging to Mimi, fastening themselves delicately only to quickly release themselves and pass on to new places.

Her breasts ached and their tips were painfully sensitive. The drink Leyra had given her was coursing potently through her veins. She had lost all will to protest. She could only lie there and feel the tendrils caressing and savoring her. They were enfolding her, exploring her, moving over her with feather-like touches. She tried to open her eyes but the lids were heavy and unwilling. She wanted to fight the tendrils, which had now reached her stomach. From somewhere a voice was speaking to her softly, soothingly. "Please, darling, don't fight me. You should know what you mean to me—to us. I'll never do anything to hurt you, dear. Please, just lie still and let Leyra—"

The voice died away. But Mimi felt the tendrils still trailing over her. This was so different from anything she had ever known. No heaviness, no hardness, no pain—only gentle, teasing meanderings.

Suddenly Mimi's body responded violently. She was like a violin, throbbing sweetly and vibrantly, with Leyra expertly plucking the strings. Mimi relaxed her body, wanting and waiting for more of the exquisite music, all gentleness and lightness and poignant ecstasy....

Hours later when she awoke, the afternoon had spent itself. Her body was warm and moist from the daytime heat. She lay still, trying to recall the odd and vague impressions of the previous night's experiences. She arose from the bunk and dangled her legs over the side. She needed a bath and things to wear. Of course she could wear the costume back to her room in the big house on the hill. It would not matter to anyone.

She opened one of the two doors in the cabin. Inside was the head. There was no tub but off to the side was a shower stall. She turned on the water and had a steaming shower. Afterwards she rubbed herself briskly until her body glowed a rosy pink. She stood in the center of the room, dripping wet, beads of water clinging to her body as she began to dry herself. A breakfast tray covered with a white, lustrous napkin caught her eye.

She removed the napkin and saw the note Leyra had left for her.

"Darling, I hope you slept well. It is very quiet in this cabin. Perhaps you'd like to lunch with me in my room in the Big House after you wake up. We can have a lovely chat. Mimi, I can't tell you enough how happy you've made both Philip and me. We both thank you from the bottom of our hearts. Philip and Griff had a talk about things. Everything will be all right. With deep appreciation and gratitude. Leyra."

Mimi sat on the bunk and re-read the note. Her head felt strange. Then full awareness struck her as by some odd clairvoyance. She didn't know what told her, but some psychic, deep-seated knowledge from eons in the past stirred within her. She was going to have Philip's child.

She lay back on the bunk, overwhelmed by the certainty. How was her life going to be changed by these strange circumstances, she wondered. She was not afraid but her heart pounded. As long as Griff was with her, she would never mind anything— even bearing another man's child!

SIX

NICK BOTHIO was angry. Some of the men sitting in a circle in the room knew it and feared him. Others who didn't know Nick well could sense his passion but had no idea of what to expect.

It was hard to say what it was about Bothio that revealed his anger. It was not his voice. He still spoke softly. It was not his manner. He was still poised, suave and disciplined. But anger flowed from him like a storm-cloud and clung to the walls of the room and engulfed the men in its threat.

In contrast to the rich lushness and elegance of the rest of the Paradise Club, the plainness of the room was dramatic. There were no upholstered chairs or sofas here. Twelve plain wooden chairs and a desk at one corner of the room were the only furniture. Even ashtrays were missing. No one smoked in the Meeting Room.

The men gathered here were the elite of the city's criminal underworld. Somebody was out to make trouble. And he, Bothio, intended to stop it before it got out of hand and became too big to control.

He had a good idea of where the trouble was coming from, but he had to first make sure. He had sent Silky out to do some digging around. The smooth-faced underling had come back with the answers—and one of the men in the room might well have special reason to be afraid.

"I called this meeting for a good purpose," Nick Bothio whispered with deadly intensity from his position behind the desk.

"One of you guys is growing too big for his britches. I'll know what's what soon!"

His soft voice was still. The only sound in the room was the harsh, deep breathing of the men. Tension mounted as they watched him intently.

"Look, Bothio! Things are going good for me downtown. Know what I mean? Trouble now would start the Feds moving, man. And that's trouble for me, real trouble. I just got out from under a tax rap—I need time. I spent real heavy bread for a fix man. Real heavy to beat that tax rap. I need time! Time, not trouble."

The speaker was a short, thickset man. His eyes were almost closed under their heavy lids and his lips hardly moved as he spoke. There was a slow quietness about him that was sinister. He looked at Bothio earnestly. "I sure would hate to see anything upset right now, man."

"Look, Sal, I don't have anything against you, but what do you expect me to do? Sit on my rear end and let some crumb, some two-by-four cheap nothing, move me out of my territory? Do you know how long it took me to build this up?" Bothio's voice was as musical as a singer's but his eyes were cold.

"Well, I don't want anything like that, man. You know what I mean? But as a favor to me—I've always been square with you— as a favor, man, go easy. I'd hate to see things upset now."

Bothio moved stiffly from behind his desk. He stood before Sal, who stopped speaking for a moment. When he spoke again, there was a new tone in his voice.

"Beside, Nick, I'm in a set-up different from yours. I don't touch the white stuff."

"You are still square with me—I think. I'll know for sure when Silky gets back," Bothio whispered with deadly earnestness. His body coiled like a wound spring let loose. "I'm not saying a damn thing—yet! But whoever is stepping on my toes gotta move off, clear off. Damn quick!"

A faint flush stained Sal's face. "You suspect me, too, man?"

Bothio's voice had risen to a chill, hoarse scream. The effect on the man was electric. Everyone tensed. The room was silent. Bothio's body was taut. He turned and pirouetted slowly. The light hanging from the ceiling glared down on his face. The high cheekbones were stretched tight and sharp against the skin, making the deep ravines on the sides of the mouth even deeper. His lips curled cruelly and twisted like a writhing serpent.

"Some sonofabitch is getting in my way! And I'm telling you right now, when I find out who it is, I'm gonna cut his heart out—"

He ranted and raved in a frenzy of uncontrollable passion. The scene was made more dramatic because, even though his voice had risen, it was still soft and somehow caressing. The circle of men was held spellbound by the awesome spectacle. Each of them knew that when Bothio reached this stage of anger someone paid the maximum price—his life. One hood coughed nervously. A high, falsetto giggle hit the ceiling hysterically.

Bothio stood poised, balanced on the balls of his feet like a ballplayer waiting to take off for home base. The stark, acrid odor of fear began to permeate the room.

"What makes you think it could be Nick?" The man who had spoken was tall and his long neck swiveled around towards Bothio like a corkscrew. Large eyes bugged out of his head. They looked as if they would drop right down on the long nose that almost met his full lips. "How do you know it's one of us? It could be anyone—even the Weasel," he whined in a nasal twang.

Bothio stared at him hard for a minute. "If I did know for sure that it was one of you in this room, he wouldn't be here long, Guppy. And you know it!"

"That's what I am saying. It could be a rival mob. It could—"

"It's most likely the Weasel," a gruff voice said from across the room. "But he's too sharp to stick his own neck out. You'll have trouble pinning anything on him."

"Sure," another spoke quickly." He most likely used guys from out of town to do the job."

"If it is the Weasel, don't worry, I'll find it out. You can bet your life on that!" The words left Bothio's taut lips and hung heavily in the room. "Silky has ways of finding things out. When he comes back, I'll know the whole damn story. Nobody is going to hijack my stuff!"

The door burst open and Silky minced into the room, a smile curving his faintly carmined lips.

"Boss! I found out who—" He stopped just inside the door and waited. Then a big grin broke his face, crinkling his large, limpid eyes. "Maybe I better tell you in private, hey, boss?"

Bothio followed him out of the door. While they were gone, the men in the circle shuffled and fidgeted nervously.

"Jeeze! I sure wouldn't want to be in that guy's shoes," someone whispered.

"Which guy?" a voice asked foolishly, with a vapid chuckle.

"The guy that crossed Nick! Who else?"

None of them were small-time hoods. Each represented crime in some major aspect and in a particular part of the city. Each used ruthless and cruel methods to keep his own control and power. Bothio's hardness did not shock them. They all used the same when necessary. But always there was a special and sinister, deadly quality to Bothio's anger that sent chills through even these callous men.

Now all except Sal and Guppy were awed into silence while awaiting the big man's return.

"Well, I don't want trouble with the cops right now," Sal said at last, raising his voice. "That would stir things up for everybody—especially me—and make it bad. Real bad. The Federal boys are poking around looking for trouble." The others agreed. "This is an election year, too. But who can stop Nick Bothio?" he asked. It was more like a statement than a question. "We just gotta convince him to hold off a while," he continued. "This is gonna be bad, man. Real bad."

"Maybe we can make a deal with him," someone from across the circle suggested.

"A deal? What kind of deal?"

"Oh, I dunno. Maybe like promising to find out who is hijacking his white stuff and sending him the proof that it's gonna stop."

Sal thought that over for a while. "It might work at that. If we knew who it was."

"Silky must have found out something. If we handle the thing from here on, maybe we can do it our way—and still satisfy Nick."

"Who do you think is behind the cross?"

Someone laughed and slapped his thigh. "Who? You ask who? Who but the Weasel? He's up to his old tricks. He tried that in Chicago until he got run out of there, didn't he?"

"Well, maybe we can talk Nick out of—"

"It's worth a try anyhow," another said. "Here he comes now."

The door opened and Bothio, trailed by Silky, entered. He stood just inside the door, frowning. Silky snickered behind him. Sal spoke quickly.

"Hey, man! The boys and I were thinking—and talking. And we gotta deal to make you. You see, we all want to avoid trouble right now. The deal is this—but first, you know who's crossin' your junk?"

Bothio's scowl darkened, deepening the lines in his craggy face. "Silky just brought the word. It's the Weasel all right. I'm gonna cross the river and get that guy and cut his ears off!"

"Hey, wait. That's just what I'm talking about. There's ways and ways of getting at guys. Your way is rough for now, man. It'll mean a gang war. Or something worse—the Feds pokin' their noses inta things. So here's what. We'll take care of the Weasel.

Me and Guppy and the boys here. Our way. Just you leave him to us. Okay? It's a deal?"

Bothio stared hard at him, unblinking. "I never needed nobody to take care of any double-crossing rat before and I don't need nobody to do it now," he snarled.

"We know you don't, man. But this is for the sake of the rest of us—the boys," Sal said clearly. And this time there was a tight edge to his voice that Bothio couldn't help but catch.

"I'll need proof that the bastard is out of the way!"

"We'll send you the proof. Okay?"

The group waited, tense and silent. The man in the far corner ceaselessly tossing his knife in the air paused and stared hard at Nick, who could feel the tension in the room pressing down on him.

How far could he go in bucking this group of warlords? There were too many to fight—even one at a time—and they were too big together. He knew when to change sides. This was the Combine. They could destroy him if he went too far. He could fight them, but even if he won, he lost.

The men watching him saw his eyes at last leave Sal's face. He walked over to the chair behind the desk.

"I don't want this screwed up," he said softly, speaking slowly. "If you are gonna take care of him, then you take care of him. But good! Or I'm gonna come in and do the job myself—my way."

"Okay! Okay, man. That's the deal." Sal looked around at the circle of men, something like pride on his swarthy face.

"You've got twenty-four hours to get him and send me proof," Nick continued.

"Okay! Okay! Okay, everybody?" Sal prodded.

One by one the men nodded and got up and left the room. For a long time Bothio sat alone behind his desk as Silky whistled sibilantly and the bright light winked down at the empty floor. He didn't know what was wrong, but a strange premonition that there was going to be trouble bothered him.

He had risen from the ranks of small-time hoods to be boss because of his ruthlessness and an uncanny ability to size up situations and handle them before they became too hot. In the last few weeks someone had been slowly cutting him down.

His couriers were being steadily eliminated as fast as he replaced them. And his deliveries were being hijacked. The attackers left no clues. Dead men couldn't talk But living ones did, and Silky had found out who was behind it. The Weasel.

Back in the beginning he and the Weasel had worked out an agreement. The river was to be the dividing line. Across the river was the Weasel's territory. This side was his. The truce had held, until now. What was going wrong? He knew for sure that the Weasel would not have dared to break the truce unless something was going on that he, Bothio, didn't know anything about.

The whole double-cross stunk like a job from the inside. Somebody close to him was trying to cut him down. He squinted into the darkness across the room.

The Combine left him a good part of the narcotics trade and lesser stuff. He hadn't been stepping on anybody's toes. But the Weasel had been up to his neck with the Fed boys recently. He had only barely managed to squeeze through without an indictment. In contrast he, Bothio, was clean. He had been smart. And lucky. The back of his neck tingled suddenly. Was somebody trying to put the finger on him? Was this the beginning of a double-cross, maybe?

He couldn't fight the Combine alone. He was going to do some look-see. He had never depended on anyone but himself for the heavy loads when they came. That was why he had reached the top.

Suddenly he clapped his hands to his head and squinted hard. His face flushed beet red. The pain hit him so hard that for a moment everything else was blotted out—his thoughts, the Weasel, everything.

"What's the matter, boss? That headache again?" Silky's lisp reached him from far away. "You want I should get Asia?"

Another wave of pain, hot and searing, slashed him. He nodded his head. Silky took him by his elbow and led him to the elevator and down to his apartment. Fiery stabs of agony were gouging into him, turning his face purple and livid. The stabs lived and grew and became one with the breath he drew in short, gasping grunts.

He didn't know he was home, stretched out in his own bed, until long afterward. Something cool was on his forehead. He lay still, expecting the hot shafts of fire to tear him to pieces, but they did not come. He opened his eyes at last and stared into the slanting green eyes of the sinuous dancer.

"Lie still now, cherie! Don't move for a while. You fainted from this one."

She lifted the cloth that had become warm. He heard running water in the bathroom and then the coolness was on his forehead once more. He relaxed and breathed out a sigh. Asia was a good kid.

"They are getting worse, aren't they?" Her husky voice reached him. He thought over the question.

"Yeah. They sure hit me a rap."

"It's as I've been telling you all along. We should pull up stakes and go away for a while for a good rest. You know, Florida or maybe even Paris. You've been killing yourself for a long time now—"

His hand waved and cut her short. "I can't take off just like that. As soon as I leave, everything will tumble like a house of cards. Who do you think is keeping all this together? Me! So now I should go away and lose everything I've spent my whole life on?" He laughed shortly. "What a life! My whole life to build for that jackal across the river! That's just what he's waiting for. The goddam vulture! The crumb!"

He threw off the silken coverlet violently and sat up. Asia protested, putting a slim hand against his chest. He pushed her away roughly.

"I can't afford to be sick. This damn pain will have to go away. Aw, Christ!"

A sudden attack made him slump over on the side of the bed. Asia quickly straightened out his legs and placed another compress on his forehead. This time he did not protest. His body began to shake as he fought the paralyzing agony.

"Want me to give you something that would make it go away right quick?"

He shook his head. "You know I only sell the damn stuff and never touch it. Think I'm crazy?" he whispered through clenched teeth. He heard her fussing about the room, felt the darkness as she turned out the light and then her soft rustlings as she sat in the chair near his bed.

He lay still, trying to force the pain away by will alone. Thoughts drifted into his mind like a soft cloud. His life. His childhood in the drab section of the Bronx. The only Italian family in a murky Jewish neighborhood. The struggle his mother had to raise five boys with no man to help.

His father had been killed one night by scabs in a dock fight while Nick was still a baby. He had grown up in the teeming Bronx streets while his mother had slaved away at the stove in the steaming kitchen of the dingy railroad flat, making spaghetti and ravioli and other Italian dishes to feed the men who worked at the big market a block away.

The money wasn't much but it had paid the rent and Mama Bothio always had something to give the boys to put in the collection basket on Sundays. She saw to it that Nick and his brother Angi went to Mass every sabbath.

Nick would sit on the edge of his seat, squeezed in between wheezing old men or gray-haired old ladies whose lips moved in sibilant whispers. With all the sincerity of his young heart, he would pray to St. Anthony that "Mamma mia wouldn't have to work so hard—"

But his prayers never seemed to be answered. At last one day, during his fourteenth year, kneeling on the cold marble before the altar rail, he prayed for the last time. His prayers were answered but not in the way he had in mind. Very quietly Mrs. Bothio died in her sleep.

Nick's childhood died with her. Overnight it seemed, just before his fifteenth birthday, he became a man. The change wasn't so much outside as inside. A stillness about him and leashed power and resoluteness showed through and frightened people, causing them to keep away from him in apprehension. There was something about his eyes, too—dead level and unblinking—that made others look away. Nick himself never realized how close he had been to his mother until the loneliness set in.

It was then that he made a strong effort to get control of the gang he'd been hanging out with. He was tough and strong and deadly with a knife. His slightest wish became a command and his power grew with the years, especially after he linked up with Benny the Gimp. But the crowd that was forever around him always left him lonelier than ever. Not even the wealth and power he later acquired relieved the haunting loneliness.

Benny the Gimp, was closer to him than anyone else. But even so, there was always that impenetrable wall between them. It was Benny who taught him to trust no one, not even him. And to drive the lesson home so Nick would never forget it, Benny one day, deliberately and coldly, betrayed him. Bothio never did forget.

Born in poverty, never knowing luxury, Nick developed as he grew a forbidding and majestic presence. Neither money nor success meant anything to him. Money he spent easily and freely to get what he wanted. It was a curious side of his nature. He wore his success like a graceful mantle. And an innate gentleness, which he held in check deep inside, developed into a polished suavity.

There was always a deadly purposefulness about everything he did. His soft voice and stillness lent such a sinister aura to his action that those close to him spread the fear and his reputation for violence grew. His ambition was power. His word was his bond. He kept his promises no matter how difficult or how lightly made. He became, through the years that followed, a rare type of hood, represented for good qualities and at the same time feared for his ruthless anger.

He had graduated, under Benny's tutelage in the early days, from petty crime to the bigger stuff. Benny had taught him how to think, how to plan and then how to anticipate trouble and cover it. Added to this was his own natural gift for organization.

Soon his area of activity had expanded and he was crimelord of the entire Bronx area. Then the Big War came, bringing changes. Instead of waiting to be called, Nick had enlisted for the service, knowing that he would have to fight to regain the control he would lose while overseas. He never doubted that he would come back.

He outlasted the war; and when he got home, the nation told him he was a hero. To him it was a big joke. He had killed because killing had become a way of life with him. From childhood the code of the streets had been beat or get beaten; kill or be killed. So what?

Back home he had found things as he knew they would be. The Weasel and Blackjack Joe had carved up the territory and were running things to suit themselves. He set about letting everybody know he was back and expected to be in control of his territory again. Things were going too good for the Weasel and he hated to let go.

Sitting around the same desk that was now in the Meeting Room, he had read and spelled out the law to the boys he had gathered about him and then sent a message to the Weasel.

"Tell that sonavabitch that I'm back and intend to take over again—right where I left off!"

The message had been delivered but the Weasel hadn't moved. So soon Biffo Tom, the Weasel's right-hand man, had been given the business. One day the Weasel opened his mail and stared down at Biffo's right hand, the one with the zig-zag scar on the index finger and the jade ring that Biffo always wore. Then later that day Biffo's body was dumped at the Weasel's back door. That opened the bloody gang war that had spelled "finis" to the Weasel's empire.

After that things were fine. Nick's activities spread. He branched out from slot machines, policy games and bookmaking into the real big-time stuff. That was when he built the Paradise Club.

Overseas he had discovered that people have interesting appetites and preferences. His discovery gave him big ideas. He made arrangements to have girls sent to him from various parts of Europe and South America. He made the right contacts and threw money contemptuously in the right directions and the rooms in the underground Place below the Paradise Club were always occupied.

It was while he was overseas that he met Asia. She was a scrawny, hungry kid, shivering in the cold on a narrow Montmartre street when he stumbled on her one night after doing the bistros. She was huddled on the curb, too cold and hungry to care what happened to her.

He had stopped and stared at her. She had the longest hair he had ever seen. The red mass trailed in long, wavy trendrils on the sidewalk beside her, covering her face, her shoulders. She sat hunched forward, her face hidden in her drawn-up knees.

He had taken his hand out of his pocket and jerked her head back roughly, pulling her by her hair. Her face was white and drawn, lips blue with cold. He had jerked her to her feet and half-dragged her to the nearest bistro and poured brandy down her throat until the color came back to her cheeks. He studied her face then in the dim light of the cafe.

It was exotic and mysterious. Green eyes, large at the inner corners, slanted sharply toward her temples. Her nose was thin and high-arched. But it was her mouth that held and intrigued him. Full, sensuous lips pouted provocatively. It was a mouth made for kissing, and as he looked at the color returning to them, he felt sap rise in him along his thighs and groin as his muscles hardened.

He had poured more cognac into her glass from the bottle on the table. "Drink it up, kid! You look as if you need it."

Her lashes fluttered at him as she opened her eyes wide. She had been too cold to protest, but now she started to speak. He stopped her.

"How old are you, anyway? You don't look older than twelve to me. What are you doing out so late?"

She stared at him. "I am fourteen. And I have nowhere to go."

Her voice was husky like mulled wine, slurred, with an entrancing, exotic accent. He could not quite place the nationality.

"Where are you from? You aren't French."

"I am French and Eurasian."

He had looked blank.

"I am half Chinese—and half French. I was born in Marseilles. My mother and I came here three months ago. She was killed in a raid and I…" Her voice trailed as tears began to flow across her cheeks and down her neck.

"Don't you have any other folks?"

"My father was a seaman on a ship. I don't know what has happened to him. I have only a grandmother in Marseilles, and she is very old."

"How have you been living—you know, getting by?" he asked, knowing the answer.

"I—I—" She stared at him. The green in her eyes deepened and she bit her lip. "I had a job dancing in a club—a girl taught

73

me how. But it got bombed out and I've—" Fresh tears started to flow. He watched her for a moment.

"C'mon," he said. "Let's get out of here."

She didn't move. She just sat and looked at him.

"Look, kid, you must know the score by now," he said roughly.

"Score?" she murmured inquiringly.

"How did you learn English?" he demanded.

"In Marseilles. From the sailors as a child and from the English girl who taught me to dance. She went away with a German soldier."

"You would do better by coming with me than by holding down that cold curbstone I found you camping on."

She stared at him, unblinking. Then she nodded. "Yes. You are right."

The next morning he dressed quietly, trying not to disturb her. She looked small and forlorn huddled under the covers.

A strange tenderness stirred him for the first time in many years. He bent and gently touched her reddish, curving brows. At his touch she awoke and stared at him. Then, seeing him half dressed, she sat up in bed, the sheet pulled about her.

"You are going?" she murmured huskily.

"Yeah. Gotta report to the base. I'll be back. The rent is paid for a week. You stay here until I get back."

She nodded mutely. He thought he read something in her eyes but it eluded him.

"You are a very kind man," she said.

"Yeah. Sure." He laughed shortly. "I know a lot of guys who wouldn't agree with you."

They were together whenever he could get away. He pulled strings and got her a job dancing in a spot frequented by GIs. She had a natural grace, and as her body began filling out, her movements became sinuous. She had imagination and worked up an interesting number with the slow rhythms of the Orient.

She spoke Chinese and several other languages fluently. She also had a quick mind and the ability to fit into his moods.

It was with her that he came to know himself and discovered his strange inability. They had been together several months when one night he felt it. She lay beside him, nestled in the covers, burrowing against his shoulders. She had blossomed and bloomed into a rounded, seductive figure. It pleased him to arouse her ardor which flamed so quickly at his slightest touch. Under his tutelage the girl-child had evolved into a woman, full-blown. Now as she nuzzled him, he felt his body quicken into passion. Whatever his mood, she could mysteriously convert him to a boiling cauldron.

He hugged her to him. She lay quivering delicately, a timid fawn, taut beneath his caressing fingers. Her shivers sent new thrills coursing through his throbbing body. He clutched her hard, towering above her, feeling her tiny body becoming submerged and lost under his bigness.

Passion flicked fiery fingertips around and about him until he was a seething volcano of unsated desire—desire that he could never appease. A harsh cry of frustration broke from him. She moved and he was alone—helpless, pulsating, tormented.

Asia sat on the side of the bed and whispered soothing, unintelligible sounds, urging him. But her ministrations could not help him. Cradled in his strength once more, she was forgotten in his desperate struggle for release from the overpowering torture. It happened time and again.

At such times he felt himself to be a tiny animal enclosed in a huge metal drum that spun rapidly. Faster and faster he spun until all perspective and reality became lost and only the overpowering quest for relief remained. The torture might last for minutes or for hours, and gradually, as the time duration increased, Asia learned to elude his clinging arms to spare herself the bruises that were sure to be left on her delicate body.

On one occasion she slipped away from him and went to stand by the window, gazing at him obliquely from under long lashes. She never wondered why he reacted so—she had not had the experience to know how other men acted in similar circumstances. She felt hot and feverish from the excitement and struggle. She went to the bathroom to douse her flushed face with cooling water. When she returned to the bedroom, he was still convulsed on the bed in his painful quest, tossing from side to side. She groped in her mind for some means to assuage his agony. He sprang from the bed in a frenzy and, with a wild oath, he swept the lamp from the bedside table. Then, picking up the table itself, he hurled it viciously across the room. Asia cowered at the window. She had never witnessed such wild anger in him before. Terror so froze her to the spot that she lacked even the will to move.

She watched, weak and helpless as he made a shambles of the furnishings. Still his strange passion had not ebbed. When he faced her, his face was red and mottled. The veins lay like cords, crisscrossing in a terrifying network about his neck and temples. His eyes stared insanely and his breath came in hissing gasps.

He lunged toward her and, like a frightened moth, she lashed out with the damp towel in her hands. At the contact, Nick stood stock still, taut and immobile. His face was raised to the ceiling as if hypnotized by something he saw there. But Asia knew he was beyond seeing anything.

Again and again panic and fear goaded her to strike at the nude figure standing frozen and rooted like an ancient, wooden image. Then, as her strokes flicked repeatedly at his taut body, a great sigh hissed from his lips. He pirouetted slowly on the balls of his feet, turning until his back was toward her.

Terror gave her actions an hysterical quality and she kept on hitting him, unable to stop, faster and faster. As if from a great distance, she heard a sighing whimper, "Please! Don't! Stop! Please!" The cry was like a chant, repeated without let-up until at last it ended in a long, drawn-out cry. "Ahhhhhhhhhhhhhhh!"

And Nick crumpled in a heap on the carpet at her feet. His face was bereft of all tension and she knew that his anguished struggle had ended at last.

When Nick returned to the States, he brought Asia with him. There was a strong loyalty that made her cling to him. The weeks in Paris alone, cold and starving, were still fresh in her mind. What would have happened to her if Nick had not found her on the curb that miserably cold night?

Sitting beside his bed now, she shivered in fear of the dismal prospect. She had heard strange stories of girls who had disappeared into Germany. Into what? No one knew. In her own way, she loved Nick but she was aware with a woman's wisdom that he needed her more desperately than she needed him.

She was the only one who could handle his odd need, and she guarded the secrets of his body as if they were her own. She was jealous of the lovely women who frequented the Paradise Club. But her dread was the invert, Silky. His slightest lisp turned her cheeks white and froze her blood. She knew he earned his name from his expert use of the silken cord which he always carried coiled in his pocket.

Their hatred for one another was fierce and mutual. She knew, too, that his feelings for Nick bordered on idolatry. Excepting herself, Silky was the only member of the coterie about Nick whose loyalty he never questioned. Silky would be happier if she were not around. She was in his way. And both she and he knew that he waited, alert and amiable, for an opportunity to remove her.

She had been with Nick during those terrible days after his discharge from the service. Those were the times when he paced his rooms, silent and grim, and here and there Asia caught snatches of conversation suggesting that so and so had disappeared.

Those were the days of struggle for him, when he fought to regain his lost empire. It was during those days of frenzied pressure and excitement that the headaches had begun. Headaches which sent seering, hot, stabbing agony through his brain, making his stomach churn and souring his vitals. Again it was Asia alone who brought relief.

As he tossed on the bed near her, she rose and went to the dresser against the wall. Then her cool fingers were on his nude body, annointing his limbs with a soothing balm. The room was dark but the scent of her perfume, rich with the East, came to his nostrils, pervading him with a strange pleasure.

She turned him over and massaged his back gently. He relaxed himself into the softness of the bed and allowed the pain in his head to possess him—drowning out all consciousness and scent and feeling. He didn't know he had cried out in agony. He didn't know anything but the smothering stabs of pain that blacked out all save their own existence.

At last tiny flicks of delight began to permeate his consciousness. As he became more fully aware, his senses grew alert and his body responded with eagerness to the towel she was brandishing.

Time began to race. He could feel his body tingling exquisitely. The surface buds of his skin were titillated. He shivered and whimpered. He could hear Asia's breath coming faster. She was wearying. He wanted to call to her, but he could not. His throat was gagged with sweetness.

Asia was tired. She had danced two shows that night. Then for hours she had sat beside him, ministering to his needs. She was now near exhaustion. Just then the door opened and Silky entered the room. He minced towards her, a smile on his carmined lips.

"Can you help me with him?" she panted. "I'm about done in and he still has his headache."

Silky fluttered his long, mascaraed lashes and his perpetual smile deepened. Suddenly something dangled from his hand.

"What have you got there?" she inquired curiously. He held up the object for her to see. "What is it?" she persisted.

He dangled the slender, writhing object before her eyes.

"I made it myself. Silk. Three strands." His fingers handled it lovingly. "This is a real work of art," he said proudly.

Asia stared at it with misgivings. It was, of course, the silken cord of death he always carried. Sensing her uncertainty, Silky's face clouded.

"I'm not going to hurt him," he said peevishly," and it will make his headache go away."

Asia shrugged. "So go ahead. Make it go away," she said huskily.

Silky went to the bed where Nick lay, shudders rippling his body. Silky raised his arm and brought it down. His face flamed and convulsed with effort and excitement. His teeth clamped down on his full lower lip and he raised his arm again.

To Nick the sudden attack of the stinging tips was a startling shock. Then, as he gave himself up to concentrating on it, he became less aware of the headache. The pain replaced the agony of the headache. This new, greater pain drove away the lesser one, until quite unexpectedly, all pain disappeared. Nothing hurt any more. He was floating out into space and a wonderful sense of euphoria suffused him. A feeling of exhilaration, thrilling and delightful, pervaded him.

He cried out and whimpered. Asia flew to his side. He clung to her hand. Flecks of foam were at the corners of Silky's mouth and he bit down hard on his under lip, wholly absorbed. Nick cried out harshly in a gutteral sound that tore from his throat, an animal sound, deeply primitive.

Silky's body arched. His raised arm lowered. Asia, clinging to Nick's hand, whimpered. The room was still. For a moment no one moved. Asia rose and went through the opened door.

Silky fell to his knees beside the bed where Nick lay, now soundly sleeping. He laid his head beside the sleeping form. Tears ran down his cheeks and raw, ugly sobs shook his body. Nick slept on, oblivious to the arms stretched out across his body and the hoarse crying that filled the room with pleading sound.

SEVEN

T O ANYONE else but Mimi, life at Forest Green would have been wonderful. Mimi found it insufferable. Were it not for the trip to town to the Paradise Club every day in the Thorntons' limousine, driven by their liveried chauffeur, she could not have stayed.

Both Griff and the Thorntons begged her to take time off from the band and stay at Forest Green indefinitely. Griff knew a singer he could get to fill in for her. But the idea was unbearable to Mimi. Singing and Griff were her life in that order.

So each night she appeared with the band and spent some hurried minutes with Griff after the show, and each morning Griff saw to it that she was driven back to the estate after work. Her relationship with him had changed a great deal in the past three months. Or perhaps, she thought, it was Griff who had changed. There was a new tension about him, an undefined excitement that she could not explain. He was putting more of himself into his work, as if he were trying to escape something.

They were alone between shows in her dressing room one night when she questioned him about it. She felt he might be upset about the deal with the Thorntons and was trying to conceal it. She walked over to him as he sprawled on the sofa, her hips swinging insolently. She sat on the edge of the seat beside him and tousled his hair. She noticed that there were tiny lines around his mouth and a restlessness in his eyes. She bent and kissed the tip of his nose.

"Griff, are you sure that you don't mind—you know—my having the baby and staying with the Thorntons? Are you still for it?"

He turned brooding eyes on her. "What? Of course I am, doll. That was the deal, wasn't it? That was the deal so what is there to beef about?"

She was disappointed. She had hoped for a different answer. Anything to show he did not really want it this way. "I know that was the deal but you could feel jealous or something, couldn't you?" she asked tremulously.

"There's nothing to be jealous about. We made a deal with them. They've deposited the money in a trust fund for you that you can have when the baby is born—or if an accident or something happens. Now you have to go through with your end of it. What else?"

His voice was matter-of-fact, distant. Mimi snuggled deeper into his lap.

"Griff, honey, do you feel the same about me? Do you still love me?" Her voice was wistful. "Because I love you even more now. You know something? That Philip guy—made me realize more now than ever—I mean after what's happened with him—I realize that I love you more than ever. Isn't that something?"

Her voice shook and she bent to kiss him. He casually turned his head away and bent to pick up his instrument lying beside him. A sigh caught in Mimi's throat. "It will be nice, won't it, honey, when we can collect the money and get away from here and get married."

Her eyes were wide on his face, pleading with him. He turned to her then. "You know, kitten, you shouldn't be pushing two shows a night the way you've been doing. Something might go wrong. I can get another singer—perhaps a male voice—to fill in until you can join the band again."

She shook her ebony curls wildly. "No, Griff. No! No! I want to sing with the band. Honest, I do. Besides, it's too soon to start worrying about anything yet."

He stood up and ran his hand through his hair distractedly and began pulling at his lip. She clung to him. "Griff! Please love me a little. It's been so—"

He tugged at his lower lip harder and kept his face averted. "Now, kitten! You always get these wild urges at the wrong times. We've got to rehearse that new arrangement now. I promised Bothio I'd start Asia on a production number this coming weekend. You know we haven't got time."

In spite of himself he couldn't help seeing her crestfallen face. Tears were in her eyes. She shook them away. "I'm only doing this for us," she cried brokenly.

Griff clutched her hand and pulled her to him. His face was tortured and twisted. "I know, kitten! Oh, baby, I know. You do understand how I feel about you, don't you? I love you more than I've ever loved any woman in my life. But—oh, I dunno." He gave a bitter chuckle, "Maybe I'm cracking up, eh?"

He bent his head and pecked her lightly on the lips and turned away, leaving the room. Mimi stood still staring after him. Something was wrong. She could feel it. But what? She knew deep in her heart that Griff loved her. But something was blocking a full union with him. If only he would talk to her. Perhaps they could figure things out together. But this way, never knowing what was eating him, was torture to her.

She called to him and hurried out. Perhaps it was something she had done. But she had only done what he himself had asked her to do. She had never been for it in the first place. She intended to find out what was wrong and set things right between them at once. Everything she was doing was for him— to keep them together. She couldn't stand it if things went wrong now.

Asia was standing in the glow of a spotlight on stage, She was wearing an exotic and elaborate headdress that looked like a pagoda built in layers. Spangles hung from every tier, sparkling and shining with the light. A tiny bra and a long skirt of sheer fabric that reached her ankles allowed every curve and angle of her body to gleam provocatively with her least motion.

Then the music began. Griff had used an Oriental motif for the background. The theme wove itself in and out, slowly and mysteriously. But the melody was the thing that caught and held Mimi's ear. It trilled and rippled and flashed and came head-on for its terrific impact, holding her spellbound.

Griff leaned on his stick, making fast riffs and fluting the melody as the band orchestrated behind him. Mimi recognized instantly that this was no ordinary arrangement. Griff had done the real thing. He had composed the music from scratch and arranged it for the instruments of the band all by himself in a short time. She thrilled, recognizing the extent of his talent. No matter what was wrong between them, this at least was wonderful. Griff was a great musician.

She forced her eyes back to the stage where Asia was making slow, sinuous movements. As the girl's body rippled and undulated slowly, her skirt moved and caressed her languorously. Her almond eyes, their shape exaggerated by make-up, were half closed, mere slits from which green sparks flicked dangerously. She was alluring and mysterious and seductive, with a strange, primeval appeal.

Suddenly the tempo of the music changed. The strains seemed to become electrified. The dancer moved in time with the music as if charged with new fountains of energy. She whirled and pirouetted and stamped her dainty feet, one at a time. Her skirts swirled about her, exposing one rounded leg and then the other with their rich, creamy thighs above. Mimi watched her, knowing the dance would be a hit.

And that night, as she watched the show from the wings between her numbers, she knew that Griff had never written more lovely music. The show was a tremendous success. People began coming to the Paradise Club just to see it—people who did not know about the added attractions in the lower rooms.

The place was becoming known for good modern jazz in the modern vein.

But down below business went on as usual and those not in the know never suspected. Bothio was happier these days, since Sal had kept his word. One day at breakfast a grisly package had been brought to him. When he opened it, the left hand of Money John, the Weasel's chief henchman, lay before him.

There was a note attached, explaining that no further proof should be needed but if any more hi-jacking did occur, Sal would assume the responsibility for stopping it if it could be traced to the Weasel's gang.

Bothio grunted and smiled coldly. He didn't expect any more difficulty but if it did arise, he was ready to cope with it himself. But how had the Weasel known when his shipments were due and by whom? It was hard to believe that there was a leak in his own organization. He had always kept things so tightly sewn up. He decided to personally hunt down the rat. His lips curled cruelly.

The rooms downstairs were humming and buzzing with activity. He walked around the circle leisurely. Over each door was a picture. No one but himself knew that by tilting the picture a certain way he coud see inside the room. Using the pictures now, he feasted on the tableaux that met his eyes. In some of the rooms men and women were playing blackjack, poker or dice. Those who preferred to be entertained differently were given accommodations graciously. The girl-imports were available. One had only to specify the nationality, color or age and one's request was presented immediately.

Still he was discontented. Something was gnawing away at him. He was a man unfulfilled. Like most impotent men, he was sure his condition was only temporary and that all he needed was a new stimulation to arouse him.

Asia was his to keep. Everything about her was mysterious and on the grand scale. She made a profession of being a woman.

Every move, every nuance, was practiced until her womanliness had become a fine art. But that was all. She had no heart. Even so, he would never let her get away from him—yet he couldn't deny his interest in Mimi. From the very first, something about her—the insolence of her walk, the childlike quality of her voice and her matter-of-fact manner—had intrigued him.

Mimi's appeal lay in her apparent innocence and open-facedness plus an honest and shameless enjoyment of her sexiness. She was what she was and she made no effort to be anything else. She was simple and uncomplicated. He wanted her. About Griff he had his suspicions and he decided to put them to a test which would bring Mimi to him.

As time had passed and Mimi's condition had become apparent, Asia had been the first to discern it. She had a woman's true instinct for ferreting out hidden truths. When she had reported this juicy tidbit to Bothio, he had mulled over it and slowly begun to evolve his plan. Then, when Griff had finally told him of his intentions to get a male singer to fill in for Mimi when she could no longer work with the band, Nick had given the matter really serious thought. Actually, it meant nothing to him one way or another. If Mimi was going to be away, Griff's music and Asia's number would pull the crowd. But now was the time to test his idea. He called Griff to his office.

"I don't care if your singer while Mimi is away is male or female. But since you're going to use a sub, why not use Silky? Did you know he has a beautiful tenor voice?"

Griff looked flabbergasted. Bothio went on quickly. "He's a true invert, you know. It's not put on for effect or anything like that. The kid is for real."

Griff had to agree to give Silky an audition. Mimi was sitting out front between numbers when Silky came on stage and took his position before the mike. That was her first inkling that a substitute had been found for her. Silky had a true, high tenor that was clear and sweet. Griff had to work hard with him but

Silky learned fast and his voice had a startlingly delightful effect on his listeners. He was an instant success.

Mimi agreed with Griff that she could not appear with the band any longer. It was July and her condition was such that she needed all the care the Thorntons agreed to foster on her for the baby's sake, or perhaps for their own sakes. Leyra and Philip were both thrilled at having her and did all they could to make her feel at home in Forest Green. She was told to make herself comfortable as she would be considered a member of the family.

At first Mimi had spent her days stretched out in a deck chair soaking up sun, wearing nothing but shorts and a bra. But as the days ran together, she soon wearied of the idleness and looked around for some other way to pass the time.

She began taking long walks in the wooded sections around the house. But she got tired of walking alone and settled down again in the deck chair by the pool. She never would get accustomed to country living, she decided.

Leyra, trying to tie her loose ends together, made many suggestions, none of which were taken. One day Mimi agreed to go down to the village with her. Perhaps the trip would break the monotony of doing nothing. She missed rehearsals with Griff and the boys and the frenzied excitement of preparing a new show and all the other uncertainties of show business. Life at Forest Green was too orderly for her.

She got into the station wagon with Leyra, moving her cumbersome body slowly. They drove through the tree-lined streets to the village. Forest Green village still boasted many historical landmarks and which proudly bore the stamp of old Captain Thornton. Leyra pointed them out to her. There was the whaling museum. Next to it was the whaling church from which all the now vanished fishermen used to march in solemn procession behind the pastor to the whaling ships lying at anchor in the bay for the blessing of the fleet.

Leyra showed her the Waiting Rock. There the whalers' women stood their lonely vigil, waiting and watching for their men to return to them. All this town history soon palled on Mimi and Leyra, sensing her mood, returned to the manor house early.

Mimi flopped on the oversized sofa with a book to read and promptly dozed off. She didn't know how long she had slept. Murmuring voices aroused her. The room had darkened and a softly shaded light was on a table near a window.

She recognized the voices as those of Philip and Leyra. They were speaking softly so as not to disturb her. Mimi tossed her legs over the side of the sofa and sat up, tousling her curls.

"Hi, you two! What time is it? I'm famished. Honestly, I've never been so hungry before in my life!"

Leyra wheeled her chair over to her. "Oh, I'm sorry I woke you, dear. You needed the rest." She placed her hand on Mimi's. "You also need to eat more. After all, you are eating for two now, you know, dear. You should be famished."

Philip looked at the two women together and a slight smile curved his lips. He joined them, sitting on the other side of the sofa with Mimi in the middle. She sat with one leg tucked under her. Her dress was pulled up over her leg, exposing the creamy thigh. Leyra caught Philip staring at the naked area. A light flush was on his face and his sensuous lips glistened where he had licked them.

She excites him, Leyra thought. She's the only woman in the world besides myself who has ever been able to do that. I wonder if he enjoyed her very much that time on the boat. She felt a warmth suffusing her. A pregnant woman is so beautiful. She remembered her own body at the early stages of her pregnancy. How excited she had been over it and how she had thrilled with a particular intensity to Philip's touch. Is she feeling that way too, she wondered.

"I think I'll go upstairs and change for lunch," she said. Then suddenly she turned back to them. Philip's hand was on Mimi's thigh. "Why don't we all go upstairs and dress? It's almost mealtime, you know." She noticed that Philip moved his hand only when Mimi stood up.

Leyra had to take the ramp which had been especially installed for her to get the second floor. Mimi reached her own room first and Leyra stared at the closed door intently before going to her room, which connected with Philip's on the left. She used her room as a dressing room, for Philip had continued to object strenuously to separate bedrooms. Mimi's room was next to Philip's and there was a connection between them that no one had ever bothered to bolt. The door was always shut but Mimi had never locked it.

Leyra took a quick shower and dressed. Afterward she wheeled herself to Philip's room. It was empty. She heard voices in Mimi's room. She listened. The connecting door was ajar. She pushed it open slightly and gasped at the sight.

Philip was on his knees beside the bed. Mimi was lying nude on the edge of the bed, her velvety skin creamy and baby pink. Her pregnancy flowed in voluptuous curves. Philip was kneeling as if in prayer, his hands stretched out before him on Mimi's body. On his face was a look of pure rapture.

Leyra felt hot green hatred mount inside her. As she watched, Philip's hands began a gentle caressing and stroking of Mimi's belly. The belly rose in a round, firm ball above the pink length of the reclining figure. Like a bloated fish, Leyra thought.

Mimi's face was flushed and she tossed her head from side to side restlessly. Slowly, evenly, Philip's hand moved over the swollen lump. It was almost hypnotic in its effect but Leyra knew that stark seething passion was incubating and discharging between the two.

She closed the door softly and stole away. When they came down to lunch, she was already eating. She broke a roll calmly and, buttering it, looked toward Mimi.

"You look so refreshed. Did you manage a shower? Philip is the one who can shower in double quick time. Can't you darling?"

She leaned over and kissed him lightly on his cheek. Then, smiling serenely, she continued eating her roll. "What are you two going to do after lunch? I thought I'd go down to the boat. It must be much cooler down there, don't you think so, Philip?"

"Oh, I don't know. When it's warm up here, it's usually warm everywhere," he answered, a frown creasing his brow.

It was a moment before she answered. "Oh, well. If you don't want to come with me, I guess Mimi can entertain you far better. She at least has two good legs."

Her voice had not lost its calm. Puzzled, Philip looked at her. She pretended not to notice and continued speaking in the same matter-of-fact voice. "You know, I'd like to have the pool drained."

"In the middle of the season?" Philip asked, truly astonished.

"I don't see what that has to do with it," she replied.

"But it was drained just a little while ago."

"So? I know that, but I would like it drained just the same. Don't you think it needs it, Mimi? You're always there."

Philip still stared at her. Mimi was looking at her with a forced smile. She's jealous, she thought. She wants to hurt me. She must have seen Philip and me in my room. But how could she be jealous. She was all for this and for my coming here. I don't get it.

Suddenly she felt homesick for Griff and the boys and show business, where people showed openly what they felt and didn't play games with each other. She wished she had never entered into the crazy arrangement or that the baby had already been born so that she could get far away from the Thorntons and return to her normal way of living. She had half a mind to get dressed and head for the Paradise Club. But she knew that she would only be in the way there and that Griff would be displeased with her. She rose from the table.

"I think I'll stretch out under that big oak near the pool and soak up some sun."

She sat supinely under a clump of shrubbery near the huge oak tree. It was quiet and peaceful. Birds were singing and the Paradise Club seemed far away. But tension was prickling in her like goose pimples. Leyra's voice still rang in her ears. She wondered why Leyra had suddenly changed. Maybe she feels that Philip is gone on me. He was kind of crazy upstairs.

It didn't much matter to her. The only man she had ever really wanted was Griff. She couldn't understand why she always reacted to Philip whenever he touched her. He had really reached her up there on the bed, she had to admit. She dismissed it as of no importance, without meaning. Just the same, she flushed while re-living the thrill and the excitement of Philip's hands on her belly and her breasts.

She didn't blame Leyra. After all, she would feel the same way about Griff. She would not be able to share Griff the way Leyra had shared Philip. She could not understand that kind of love. But since Leyra was getting green-eyed, maybe people were basically all alike after all.

Philip came out in bathing trunks and headed for the high diving board. She watched him lazily as he mounted the steps and stood poised before taking the dive. He is a good-looker, she thought, except for his mouth and he looks so much like Griff that in the dark—. She watched Philip make his dive and swim vigorously across the pool.

"He is really quite a wonderful person, Mimi. Weak, yes. But wonderful." Leyra had wheeled up beside her and was looking down on her now. Her eyes were lit strangely. "I suppose to outsiders we seem strange here in Forest Green. We don't mix much. Only with the same people we knew as children—grew up with—who think like we do. I hope you haven't acquired a bad impression from all that's happened."

Mimi turned her head lazily. She was bored by the chatter. "I've been in show business all my life. I've seen a lot of queer things. Nothing fazes me now, so don't worry about me."

"I don't think we are making you feel at home, somehow," Leyra persisted.

"I'd feel better if this were all over with but I'm all right. Forget it and stop worrying about me." She realized that she had spoken sharply but it did not seem to matter.

Leyra stared at her piercingly and then shifted her eyes to Mimi's creamy thighs where the cloth was pulled taut over her firm buttocks. Her hands fluttered on her lap. Both remained silent, looking at Philip as he approached them, water dripping from his body and falling in glistening drops on the grass.

His body was sun-bronzed to a rich, creamy gold that contrasted strikingly with his silver-gold hair. The muscles on his thighs and torso rippled rhythmically as he moved. In spite of herself, Mimi felt herself grow warm. If only Griff were here!

She buried her head in her folded arms to blot out the sight but she couldn't dispel the inner excitement. She was so easily excitable these days. Now that she needed Griff most, he was not accessible to her. Discontent pervaded her. The reckless mood that was becoming more and more undeniable possessed her.

That evening at dinner she asked Leyra to change her room. She thought one further down the hall would be better. The other woman looked at her with wide eyes.

"But why do you want to change? That's one of the most comfortable rooms in the house. Besides, if you should need anything at night, we are right nearby."

Mimi was silent at the other's argument. She could not deny the logic but she had a feeling that there was something behind Leyra's insistence on her occupying the room. Later she telephoned Griff at the club and could not reach him. He was in rehearsal with Silky, the voice at the other end told her, and nobody could disturb him. Orders.

She hung up the phone disconsolately. She would run over to the Club tomorrow. She felt completely out of sorts. A thunder storm was coming up and the atmosphere was heavy and oppressive. The air smelled different, too. Her body felt moist and uncomfortable. She stripped off her clothes and fell across the bed.

It must have been very late when she awoke. The room was pitch black and she could hear rain falling and lashing against the windows. The storm raged in heavy fury as only late summer storms on the coast can do. But it was not the storm that had awakened her. Someone was in the room. She lay still, listening. The carpet muffled the footsteps but she felt someone's presence near. Then strong hands were on her body and she knew. Philip.

She pretended to be asleep. Philip's groping hand touched her face. A stab of lightning revealed him as he bent over her. Then his hand was on her chest, massaging her heavy, sensitive breasts. She bit her lip to keep from crying out. The hand wandered to her rounded belly, caressed it tenderly, then rose to her breasts again. The nipples stood erect, hard and rigid. They were always turgid these days. She felt her knees contract involuntarily as her body became charged with fire.

Her movement stimulated him, opening the valve of his dormant passion. With a tiny moan he began kneading and fondling the voluptuous body. Philip's desire for Mimi was new and frightening in his own eyes. He had never overcome his shyness with women except with Leyra. They had been married just about a year when she had the accident that limited their physical life together. Now only Mimi could release the dam of his pent-up emotional life.

Living in proximity to him and carrying his child, she was a challenge that many men far more experienced than he would have found hard to ignore. Philip, held in limbo with his true love for Leyra on one hand and the newly awakened passions for Mimi, the mother of his unborn child, on the other, was in continuous torment.

Mimi knew with clear-sighted logic that she was not in love with Philip but, needing Griff, she found the man an acceptable substitute, particularly in that psychological frame of mind which many women experience during pregnancy. She needed someone to love her at this time, to pay attention to her, to arouse her and yet to exalt her in the ideal state of motherhood.

If Griff had been available, ardent and attentive, she would have clung to him instead. But he was a distance away, his own personal confusion coming to a head now that Silky was singing with the band. He was psychologically at the threshhold of self-discovery and his still unconscious knowledge disturbed him. For that reason, he wanted Mimi out of the way, even while feeling fondly toward her. Griff literally didn't know himself.

Sensing his rejection, Mimi turned to Philip. And Leyra, rejected for the first time in her marriage, was becoming really frightened. Philip gave himself up wholeheartedly to his passion for Mimi. No longer were inhibitions restraining him.

The child gave him confidence. Mimi was the mother of his child stirring within her. He could feel the movements with his hands. And this mutuality with Mimi excluded Leyra. Philip, without knowing it, was attempting to share in the glorious miracle of life. By touching and fondling Mimi's swelling body and identifying with her as her body changed day by day, he became a vicarious part of the process. But Leyra could not know this and fretted while silently pretending a calm that she alone knew was false.

Tonight Philip's need for Mimi had been so great that he had crept from Leyra's side to Mimi in the next room. Mimi turned, seeking a more comfortable position. Philip could feel her back pressing into his chest as he cradled her to him. Her full hips bored into the curve of his legs.

It was so good and safe to be held like this, Mimi thought, her despondency temporarily disappearing. She could feel Philip's tension as he stiffened against her. His arms felt like iron bands about her. She pushed herself hard against him, boring into him, trying to lose herself in him. His maleness was now her strength. She could feel his chest against her back.

Then the night exploded into a thousand myriad stars of various colors that flickered and sparkled, enveloping her in a blinding, thrilling incendiary of emotion. Again and again she felt as if she were whirling faster, ever faster, flying high in the sky as stars whirled about her. Her breath came in pants and gusts and consciousness all but left her. As from a great distance, she heard Philip's voice. He was calling her name as if in mortal agony, but she knew that the agony was only the very same sweet pain that she was feeling.

Her breath caught in her throat and the agonies of wanting and receiving and giving mixed and blended together. Just as she was about to cry out in ecstasy from the joy, the beauty of the moment, trying to reach the lovely stars, she felt a gentle hand on her body.

Soft fingers brushed her hip. The stars wavered in their flight, halted but gathered momentum again as Leyra's touch gently fanned them on their way. Leyra now joined the search for the showering red, blue, green and yellow stars.

At last, after eons of time and the fall of millions of stars, Mimi returned to earth. She was wonderfully weary and relaxed and soon found profound and peaceful sleep ...

As the days passed, no one referred to Leyra's presence in Mimi's room on that never-to-be-forgotten night.

With her natural insouciance, Mimi easily threw off Leyra's strange actions and moods. There were days when Leyra was as gracious as she had ever been. Then on other days she would snap and pout and would be at Mimi like an ill-tempered cat. Philip, manlike, held aloof. As the season advanced and the days grew shorter, so did Mimi's temper. She was anxious and impatient to be back at work, to be with Griff and the boys of the band, to feel the audience responding to her as she reached out to them from the bandstand.

EIGHT

THE KNOCKING had been going on for some time before Griff heard it. He had fallen asleep at the piano in his apartment and the morning sun streamed in through the open windows. The bright glare showed up the disorder of the room. He got up stiffly and limped to the door.

Silky stood smiling at him. He was debonair, with his long hair smooth and slick. His limpid eyes warmed at sight of Griff.

"Hi, Mac! Thought I'd have to come in through the keyhole. What's cookin?"

As he passed, Griff caught a whiff of perfume that lingered in the air. Silky minced over to the piano, his hip movement pronounced now that he was away from public view. Sheet music was everywhere, littering the floor, lying on the chairs and scattered over the tables. The ashtrays overflowed with stale butts.

"Your arrangement." Griff waved his arm tiredly.

"Oooh! Ducky!" Silky cooed, clasping his hands before him. "I love those wonder-derful arrangements you've been making for me, honey," he lisped. "But this place is a mess. Mind if I tidy up a bit? I can't stand a dirty, disordered place."

Griff fell in a chair without answering. Silky's eyes narrowed. "Been up all night?"

"Yeah. What day is this?"

Silky went about the rooms emptying ashtrays, straightening disordered cushions and stacking sheet music in a neat pile beside the piano. Griff sat on the sofa looking at him through heavy-lidded eyes. He was bone tired and dark circles shadowed his eyes. His face was rough and dark with an unshaved stubble.

"Wednesday, honey. You really are beat, aren't you, sweetie?" Silky answered.

"What's with the Club these days?" Griff asked wearily. He had not been there during the three days he was working on the new arrangements for the new show. Now that Silky had replaced Mimi, Griff had to get the new numbers ready for the surprisingly good tenor that Bothio's chief assistant had proven to be.

"Oh, nothing much. Nick's fit to be tied these days. He says there's a leak in the organization and he's really out to find the stoolie. I wouldn't want to be in that guy's shoes when he does."

Silky stared at Griff who sat unmoving, the cigarette burning close to his fingers. His face was slack and his mouth was open vacantly. Silky's eyes narrowed. Then he smiled and minced over to Griff. He dropped to his knees before him and gently removed the burning cigarette stub from his fingers.

"You're all done in, honey. Working so hard for me," he whispered.

Griff was in shorts and a rumpled shirt whose collar was grimy with dirt. His sleeves were rolled up. Silky began to gently caress the smooth skin of Griff's arm.

"Let me make you relax, honey. Silky knows how to make you relax real nice," he whispered.

Griff's body flinched involuntarily at the first contact of Silky's hand on his arm. His half-shut eyes fluttered open and then tiredly closed again. Shudder after shudder shook his body and a sigh escaped his opened lips. He was too tired to think, to reason or to feel revulsion.

He sat passive, allowing the new strange feeling of excitement and peace steal over him and lull his throbbing nerves. Getting a new show ready was always hectic. Always Mimi had always been with him before to share the burdens and to ease some of the tensions. He would not let himself admit that he missed her sorely. He had come to feel that Mimi was a part of him in the two years they had been together.

He was eager to have her back after the baby came, and though he would never think of admitting this to her, he hated her being away. It never occurred to him to wonder why the fact that Mimi was having a child for another man never bothered him.

Silky's presence in the band had taken up some of the slack. The slim henchman had a way of making himself useful and becoming indispensable. Perhaps that was how he had wormed his way into becoming Nick's second in command.

Griff felt his head being forced back on the sofa and against a pillow. His legs were stretched out and his shoes removed. Then cool hands were stroking his forehead and time passed as he slept the dead sleep of the completely exhausted. When he awoke, the room was tidy and neat and good smells were coming from the kitchen. Through the windows he could see that night had fallen. He opened his eyes and sat up. His eyes burned and felt gritty.

He got up and staggered over to the cupboard and poured a stiff hooker of whiskey in a glass and gulped it down. After the drink he felt better but the taste of the liquor lingered in his mouth. He started over to the sofa, then turned back and grabbed the bottle and took it with him as he fell heavily on the sofa. By the time Silky came out of the kitchen, the bottle was half empty.

"Goodness! Aren't we overdoing it a teeny weeny bit, honey?" Silky said, noticing the bloodshot eyes and haggard face. "A good hot shower is just what you need. Then I'll give you a good massage and a cold shower after. And you'll feel like new!"

Griff heard him as if from far away. He was floating in limbo and nothing mattered. Not Silky, not Mimi. Nothing. It was a vague world of drifting forms and slow movements where nothing was real. Not even the hot and cold shower and the strong, vigorous massage brought him fully awake.

He was only half aware of hands touching his body and, as if in a dream, another person whom he took for Mimi slept beside him. But there was a difference in the feel of the touch and something disturbed him so that in his sleep he tossed and moaned fitfully and couldn't really rest.

The following days brought a subtle change in Griff which was hard to define. He rehearsed the new show with an intensity that kept the men in line and precluded any nonsense from them. The group was so tired at the end of the sessions that they could only sullenly flop about the room on the chairs and try to relax.

Tubby was edgy and getting edgier. He was explosive material. He had finally become really troublesome. He couldn't get enough of the drugs he needed so vitally even though huge quantities of it were around. He had to make trips to the city for it and he hated traveling.

With Griff working him so hard and keeping herd on him, he hadn't been able to get away as often as he needed to and for the past two days he had been on short supply. He had tried to get some of the stuff from Nick's stock but hadn't been able to swing it.

Everyone was afraid of breaking Nick's rule that he enforced ruthlessly. No one who worked in the Club was allowed to buy from him. He never used drugs himself and never encouraged his workers to do so. This wasn't because he was overflowing with morality or solicitude. It was simply self-protection.

Anyone on the stuff was a potential canary and could not be trusted. He wanted no stool pigeons in his organization or close to home base. Griff spent more time than he could afford keeping Nick from finding out that Tubby was a main-liner.

Just as they started leveling off on one of the big numbers of the show, Tubby grew fretful. He was beating on the ivory, setting the rhythm for the number Silky was singing. Tubby did not like Silky and he showed it. He delighted in imitating the smooth-talking hood because it always got a rise from him.

Nobody else seemed to irritate Silky as Tubby could. Now he started to vent his nervousness on the singer, who was standing on stage before the microphone waiting for his cue to begin the last chorus of the number.

Griff had been pushing them hard and they were jittery. Tubby deliberately missed his beat, changing the rhythm just enough to throw off the inexperienced singer. Then the band was playing but Silky was lost, straggling along, trying to keep up but failing dismally.

Chink looked across at Tubby who winked at him and smiled. Chink kept on playing. Silky struggled, stopped, then bravely began again. But he couldn't get back on line with the music. He stopped and stamped his foot, his face red with anger.

"Why don't you silly boys keep in time? How can I sing when you don't play the music right?"

Tubby snickered. "Who's talking? If you'd read the music, you'd be able to sing the song the way it's supposed to go."

"You know I can't read music. I sing by ear," Silky stormed. "You're doing that deliberately to torment me. You don't like me. That's what!"

He burst into tears and ran over to Griff and fell sobbing on his shoulder. Griff turned pale. He pushed Silky away but the singer clung to him, weeping loudly. Griff was frozen from confusion and chagrin. His face was a cold mask. He thrust Silky away savagely. The singer staggered back and fell sprawling on the stage. Tubby and Chink guffawed more out of malice than amusement.

Asia, who had entered the stage unseen, crossed quickly and started to help Silky to his feet. He pushed her away crossly. "Don't you touch me! You female!" he screamed. "This is between Griff and me."

He got to his feet and dusted himself off and, with head held high, left the stage. Asia turned to Griff.

"You were awfully rough with him. He won't forget that." Her usual inscrutable smile was on her lips. "I know him. He is vindictive."

"What the hell do I care about his vindictiveness?" Griff spoke every bit as crossly as Silky had done. He despised himself for the excitement the touch of the singer had aroused in him.

To hide his trembling, he yelled harshly at Chink and Tubby. "You two know better than to mix your personal feelings with business. Tubby, the next time you do a thing like that, you're through!"

Tubby's eyes went flat and his fat chin quivered with indignation. "That's okay with me, man. To tell the truth, I don't like the pitch you been putting down. You been acting mighty queer lately. And I mean queer!"

Griff glared at him. "Just what do you mean by that crack?" His voice was deadly.

Chink, seeing that things were getting rough, came between them. "Aw! Cut it out. Cut the jazz, you two. We'd better get back to work if we want this shop to open on time or Bothio will be giving us the heave-ho. And I, for one, like it here."

Tubby went back to thumping softly on his piano and after a moment Griff quieted down. He was still in a ferment, not so much from Tubby's remark as from the strange feeling that Silky's touch had stirred in him.

He went over to the side of the room and pulled out a hip flask and took a long draw from it. He had taken to drinking lately during rehearsals, something he had never done before. His left eyelid twitched uncontrollably. Nothing he did stopped it.

He picked up his clarinet and blew a few riffs and then held a long one. He was blowing as good as ever, if not better. There was a new intensity in his playing, a feverish tension that gave depth to the music but left him unsated and restless. For the first time he could find no ease in playing. He began the rehearsal anew, driving the men mercilessly.

Asia's show number was built around a full chorus of dancers. The girls were rehearsing in a large room known as the

Conference Room. The exotic Asia, still in her tights, gazed at Griff silently for a time, her slitted green eyes unblinking.

"I came to tell you that the girls are ready for the dress rehearsal."

The show was opening in three days and nothing was going right as far as Griff was concerned. Never had he worked with a show that was so out of joint.

"Has the scenery come yet?" he asked her curtly.

Asia shrugged her shoulders eloquently. "I've been rehearsing all morning. I wouldn't know."

"Nobody else around here does either," he answered. "Where the devil is Jake? You can never find that prop man when you want him. Hey, Jake!"

Asia watched Griff's retreating figure with a quiet, Mona Lisa smile. Tubby stared at her for a moment. She was some dish. Different. He liked slim women. They balanced his bulk. Had he not been so edgy from drug hunger, he might not have been bold enough to do what he next did.

"Hey, babe!" he called softly.

Asia turned slowly to face him. She looked him over without changing the expression on her face, yet somehow she gave out a feeling of such scorn that Tubby blanched. He heard Chink's low warning.

"Down, boy!" Chink cautioned. "Off limits for you and me, pal. See and don't touch. Papa no like."

Tubby was still grinning foolishly at the girl who looked up at him impassively. Did he read an invitation in those slanting, mysterious eyes? Flecks of light came and went. It must be the lighting, he thought, and reluctantly turned away. But tiny fingers were still inching down his spine and his groin.

Griff walked through the maze of circular rooms that was the Place, trying not to get lost in looking for the prop man, Jake. This was a weird place, all turns and curves. It was a major project to find the room you wanted. You needed a floor plan or a map. He seethed silently.

Then suddenly he stopped short and gasped. He was in an open foyer with doorways radiating like arms from its four sides. The doors were closed to the right and left of him but directly in front of him the door was ajar, as if carelessly pushed by someone and not completely closed.

He could not see inside the room but a mirror was so placed on the opposite wall that it reflected the two occupants, although no features were visible.

As he stood immobile, voices came to him in sibilant whispers. Did he recognize the voices? Did that heavy trembling voice belong to—? He couldn't be sure. Then, as he groped in his memory, one of the voices laughed and Griff knew from the girlish giggle that it belonged to Silky. The singer had found sympathy for his wounded pride, but from whom?

He was about to leave when words reached him that caused him to go rigid and cold. There was no misunderstanding what was going on inside. A slow flush suffused his face. He wanted to leave but something held him fast. The words were coming to him distinctly.

Silky was crooning in gentle tones. Then the other voice answered softly. Suddenly a figure appeared in the mirror. It was Silky. The singer stood still and raising his arms above his head, he stretched luxuriously. Muscles on his wide shoulders rippled and danced as if alive. The light reflected on the slim waist and the narrow buttocks quivered and grew taut. Well-formed, slender legs curved away from the slim hips.

As Griff stared as if hypnotized by Silky's body, he felt himself grow warm. Again he felt the same odd excitement that always permeated him when the singer was about.

Yet, as he became aware of this hunger, he rejected it. And he immediately became filled with shame and self-loathing. He felt deep disgust. The muscles of his thighs were still crawling. A slow itch was inching its way up his spine. A strong desire to join the pair in the room upset him. He clung to the door frame as beads of perspiration gathered on his face.

"Oh, dear God. No! No!" he cried out in anguish. His fist beat a fierce tattoo on the wooden panel. "No! I'm not one of those. I am not. I am normal!"

The cry was wrung from the depths of his being. The truth was pressing hard at his consciousness, but it was too hard to bear. The idea that he might be different, abnormal, appalled him.

He had spent most of his years with music, sublimating his normal drive into creative channnels. Abnormality was something that other people had—not he. The idea that he could be abnormal in any way was strange and painful.

He had often sensed that something was missing in his relationship with Mimi but he had truly cared for her. They got on well together. He had become accustomed to being with her and fencing off her physical embraces, thinking her overly ardent. But now he knew. He had never really wanted Mimi. That want was what had been missing all along.

He had desired only to play with her like a sister. That was why he hadn't minded Philip and the baby. It was not the money at all. He was relieved to no longer be the one to appease her sensual needs because he knew instinctively that he could not. Now he knew what he was. He was a freak! With an anguished cry, he staggered away from the door and out of the Club.

The following morning when Silky knocked on his door, Griff's appearance shocked the singer. His eyes were red, bloodshot and sunken in his haggard face. He had not shaved and a heavy beard covered his chin and jaws. A lost, forlorn expression gave his face an odd appeal.

Griff was indeed lost and confused. He felt himself to be an outcast, a pariah. Recalling the aspersions he had heard others make about people showing the slightest deviation, he now felt himself despicable.

Silky had come looking for him when he had failed to show up at the Club. With innate wisdom Silky remained silent, staring at him. Without being told, he sensed immediately what had happened but he did not know how it had come about.

There was about the musician a new, indefinable quality that hung about him like an aura. Instead of offering sympathy, the singer was jubilant. He had, after all, always felt that Griff was one of his kind. His latency had to become active some day.

Silky minced into the room and looked about him. Empty liquor bottles were scattered everywhere. The place was in chaotic confusion.

"My! You do have a talent for messing up a place, don't you?" he asked softly. There was a new tone in his voice. He did not have to play-act any longer. "First I'll make you some breakfast and while you're eating, I'll tidy up a bit."

He gave Griff a searching glance. "There's no need for pretending any more, is there, honey?" he asked coyly. Then, before Griff could answer, he tripped to the kitchen and began banging things around.

"You know, after you left the Club, Tubby and Chink got into a fight. Man, that Tubby sure packs a fast, mean wallop," he exclaimed from the kitchen.

"What happened?" Griff asked, surprised. "Why, Chink is usually very easy-going."

"Well, not this time, he wasn't. And would you know who it was over? Asia, no less!"

"Asia? Bothio's girl?"

Silky nodded his head. Griff had come to the door. "Can you imagine that? Tubby was making a play for the doll and Chink got mad—why, nobody knows, unless he wanted to cut in— and sailed into Tubby. Honey, I mean really sailed into Tubby. Brother, was that a beaut of a fight!" Silky was enjoying the fight all over again. "It took two men to break them up."

Griff held his head and wailed. "Well, that's the end of the show."

"No. It isn't either. Bothio wanted to can the whole thing but Asia put her pretty little feet down and said she had worked like a dog and intended to open as planned and Bothio gave in but, boy! Those two really came close to Judgment Day!"

Silky stuck his head out the kitchen door. "Bothio told them to cut out as fast as and as soon as the show closes, whenever that will be. Tubby said he was ready now, but Asia talked him out of leaving. He's been ready to go anyhow 'cause he can't get his stuff so easy out here."

The singer was full of importance. Griff, remembering the trouble Tubby had been causing him lately, agreed that Tubby would have to go soon anyway.

"I'd better get out there, right away," he said uneasily. He felt guilty for having left the boys stranded two days before opening night.

"No, you're not, honey. Not until you've eaten and cleaned yourself up right. After all, we've got to stick together, don't we?" Silky asked slyly.

Griff frowned. "Cut out that damned foolishness," he growled.

But Silky only smiled. He brought out a steaming platter and set it on the table. Then he brought cups of coffee. Griff realized suddenly that he had not eaten in twenty-four hours or more.

"What got into you anyway? What gives with the run-out powder?" Silky asked. His eyes had a sly and knowing look.

"I—I—I just had it. That's all. I had to get away by myself," Griff lied.

"You sure give yourself a beating, don't you, honey?" Silky's voice throbbed with assurance. "You don't give yourself half a chance." He was still staring at Griff with a strange, intent look. "So what if we're different. Lots of people are different in lots of ways," he said slowly, looking hard at Griff.

Griff glanced up from the dirty dishes piled on the table. His eyes had suddenly become hard and glassy. "I am not a freak!" he exclaimed in an ugly voice.

Silky smiled crookedly. "Nobody said you were—but you," he answered pointedly.

Griff was too upset to notice that the feminine mannerisms had all but disappeared from the singer now. Instead there was a quiet purposefulness about the slim henchman.

"After all, there are other things much worse than what we need," Silky continued matter-of-factly.

Griff was shocked. It was one thing to admit his suspicions last night to himself and another to hear someone else voice them. His face flushed crimson and he rose from the table, knocking over some of the dishes.

"You goddammed freak!" he shouted passionately. "What do you mean by that crack? I don't have anything in common with you."

He was beside himself with rage—a rage that he really felt against himself. He raised a fist and smashed with all his might at the head of the singer sitting beside him.

But Silky was not Bothio's second in command for nothing. He had not taken his eyes away from Griff for an instant. He ducked just as the blow fell. It glanced off his cheek, landing on his shoulder. He twisted his body and his arm moved so swiftly that Griff afterward could not recall the motion. The next moment Griff was sprawling on the floor, his chest heaving, sucking air in dry gasps through his bleeding mouth.

Silky stood over him. His soft manner was coiled about him like a snake ready to strike. His tongue flicked in and out of his mouth as he hurled one insult after another at Griff.

"You crazy, stupid lunkhead! Who do you think you are? You'd dare to call me a freak? Why you're a bigger freak than I'll ever be. I am proud of what I am. I am no phony. But you! You are only pretending to be what you are not. We had your number from the time you first came here. Everybody could see how you treated Mimi. Why would a man do that to a tasty dish like that tomato if he's not a freak? And that deal you made for her. It stinks a mile long and a yard wide!"

Griff crouched at his feet, breathing hard. His chest hurt. He could only think about the show and wonder if he would ever be able to play again. Never before had he felt such pain. There was a sickness inside of him that was not physical. He felt choked with nausea. Suddenly he wanted Mimi but he knew that he could never again have the same relationship with her. His body shook with sobs as he crouched on the floor.

The anger ran out of Silky just as fast as it had come. He bent down to Griff and began to rock him gently.

"You big goof! Why did you make me hit you? Silky doesn't want to hurt you, honey. I could've killed you. Silky loves you. But you pushed me too far. If it wasn't for me, Bothio would never have signed you and the boys on. But I liked you the first time I saw you. Now let's be friends," he said, helping Griff to his feet.

Griff allowed himself to be led to the sofa. He did not care what happened to him. Everything had collapsed. The world looked a different place. He reached for the bottle just as he felt Silky's hand on his arm, inching further along the biceps. How gentle his touch is, he thought. Just like a woman's. He wondered how Mimi was getting on. He lifted the bottle to his lips and took a long swallow.

NINE

A T THE TIME Griff was wondering about Mimi, she was standing by the swimming pool at the Thornton estate. It was becoming increasingly difficult for her to move around as the child grew large within her. She was also cross and impatient all the time.

The atmosphere at Forest Green was no longer serene and peaceful though there was no tangible evidence of any change in the relationship of the three people who lived there. Mimi, who was not one to speculate about the future, sensed the tension in the air and was restless to leave.

Still, she had to stay to see the arrangement through to the end. Anyway, she told herself with satisfaction, that was not so far away. She looked at the diving board longingly and slowly sat down on the marble edge of the pool to dangle her legs in the water. The water was cold from the occasional frost which had appeared now that autumn had arrived.

The child was only three months away but these last few weeks dragged exasperatingly. She saw Philip coming toward her. How like Griff, she thought, and her longing for the absent musician crushed her spirits.

By the time Philip reached her, crossness furrowed her brows and cheeks. He stood above her and smiled. "The bloated Venus," he whispered.

Mimi's violet eyes flashed and her pout lengthened. Philip, sensing her mood, dropped lightly beside her, silent. He was not a thinking man. His simplicity was often mistaken for depth and, in reality, he had few wants and nearly all of them had been satisfied before he met Mimi. His need for her, now that she was carrying his child, was a puzzle to him—but he accepted it in his typical, nonchalant fashion.

The subtle friction that was ever present between Leyra and Mimi was all the more confusing to him. He knew that his feelings for Mimi were not love, certainly not what he felt for Leyra at least. He would always love Leyra but he was drawn to Mimi by an attraction he could neither understand nor ignore.

Philip had never heard of the deep and subtle attraction that a normal man feels for a woman who is carrying his first child. His love for Leyra would have deepened had she been the one to bear his child rather than Mimi.

Leyra fought against the feelings of jealousy that had flooded over her. Of the three, she was the most astonished at herself. She felt that Philip still loved her, although she had not thought it possible that another woman could ever move him as Mimi had. She loved him as much as ever, but the biological compact between Philip and Mimi left her out.

From her bedroom window she watched them at the poolside. She had recently taken to spying whenever she could. She hated herself for doing it, but in spite of her good intentions to stop, she continued it just the same. Philip never knew, as he cuddled her close to him at night, how she seethed with fear and torment. Nevertheless, the thought of divorce did not enter her mind. She knew he would never let her go.

It was abysmal torture to share his biological life. She admitted to herself that it was not only his interest in Mimi that upset her. It was also the repudiation she felt because of the unborn child. When Philip was with Mimi, he seemed to have no need of her.

As she looked out the window, she saw Philip bend toward Mimi and kiss the back of her neck. Leyra felt a sharp pain cut her. Her feelings were confused and her head hurt. Her head had been hurting a lot lately. She buried her face in her hands and tried to still the mad beating of her heart. The throbbing in her head made her dizzy. She felt sick in her stomach and wondered if she was going to be ill. Philip's face, as he caressed Mimi's swollen belly, came before her.

A wave of nausea swept over her. She wheeled herself to the bathroom and retched violently. Afterward she washed her face and brushed her teeth. Her face looked greenish in the mirror. Her eyes were wild. She wondered what was happening to her. Was she losing her mind? She leaned her head back against her chair and wept just before blackness overcame her.

When she opened her eyes, Philip and Mimi were standing over her. Philip was worried and trying hard not to show it. Mimi was holding a damp cloth to Leyra's lips. It was cool and comforting. She spoke soothingly.

"Here, now, honey. You just lie still while I cool you off a little. I think it's the heat that got you, eh?" Her voice was low and vibrant with concern. Leyra looked at her and smiled.

"Are you all right now, dear?" Philip asked softly. "Do you want me to get the doctor?"

Leyra turned her eyes away from Mimi and looked at him. She forced a smile. "No, darling. I'll be all right now. I think Mimi is right. It must have been the heat."

She was astonished that her voice was so calm. She straightened up, propped herself on the sofa and surrounded herself with pillows.

"You haven't been looking well lately." Philip was unconvinced. "I've noticed how pale and thin you've become. Are you sure everything is all right now?"

Before she could answer, he slipped down on his knees beside her and buried his head in her lap. "Oh, Leyra! If anything should happen to you, I don't know what would happen to me!" he cried brokenly.

Mimi's hand reached out and rested on Philip's shoulder reassuringly before Leyra could answer. "She's all right, honey. It's just the heat."

Leyra felt herself flush. She wanted Mimi to touch her. She wanted that soft, small hand with its tapering fingers and long blood-red nails to caress her body. She admitted to herself that she had felt no real desire for Philip since Mimi had come to live with them, carrying his child ... the child that she, Leyra, should have been carrying. She was jealous of Mimi. But was it because of the child, or because her husband could find delight in this girl's body rather than in hers, Leyra's—or was it because she coveted the very delights that Philip was getting from Mimi?

Leyra realized that she was following a warped line of thought, that she was succumbing to unnatural desires as she had two or three times before in response to Mimi's overpowering seductiveness. But the girl's appetizing flesh was so delectable, and exhuded such vibrant, animal attraction, that it was irresistible not only to men, but to women; so Leyra told herself.

Mimi was standing before her now, the voluptuous body only scantily covered. The white silk halter was straining against the full, mellow breasts. The ridiculous bikini that Mimi still insisted upon wearing despite her condition showed her figure heavy and distended. The girdling silk had slipped a bit too low, displaced by the bloated belly. The luscious thighs, bronzed by the sun were covered with a golden furze of fine-spun hair.

"I'm going to call Dr. MacDingle," Philip said. "You've got to be looked at, Leyra. You take care of her, Mimi," he added, and strode off.

Leyra was happy to see him go. With the cunning of madness, she asked that Mimi push the wheelchair to the bedroom.

"Help me get under the covers, Mimi," she wheedled. "And get these clothes off me, will you, dear?"

Mimi hastened to oblige. At the moment, she was full of pity for this poor, crippled creature. With Leyra propped against the bedboard, Mimi removed Leyra's blouse, her bra, her skirt. She covered Leyra with a sheet.

"Please, Mimi," Leyra urged. "I'm so jittery. Stroke my hair. Sing to me. Maybe I'll fall asleep."

Mimi stretched out on the bed beside Leyra. An old lullaby came to her lips. She fondled Leyra comfortingly as she would a child.

But Leyra was far from relaxing. Actually, she was shaking all over. Shaking not with illness, but with desire. Why should Philip have this delectable girl all to himself? Leyra wished fiercely that for an hour she could be a man! She let her hand fall stealthily on Mimi's leg. Since Mimi made no motion to push the fingers away, Leyra began to caress, as if returning Mimi's fondling. But in another moment or to, driven to desperation by the feeling of the other's flesh, Leyra threw off all dissimulation. "Mimi!" she cried. "I want you! I want you!" And she pressed herself to Mimi's luxuriant bosom.

Mimi tried to evade the attack. Yes, she had succumbed to Leyra's unhealthy advances on occasion, but only because she had been helpless or half-conscious or not in her right mind. Such abnormalities were entirely abhorrent to a girl of Mimi's healthy appetites and instincts. She pushed and scratched at Leyra—but the crippled girl, with surprising strength, managed not only to hang on tightly, but to continue her feverish caressing, at the same time kissing Mimi's skin. Leyra, who perforce had taught herself to be expert in ways of excitation and arousal, soon had the better of the battle. With a sigh, Mimi abruptly ceased fighting. However evil she considered the temptation, she had to succumb to it now. Her one inexorable need was deliverance from the torture of desire that Leyra was inflicting upon her mercilessly.

Together, lips to lips and flesh to flesh, the two women assuaged their torment. But when their writhing bodies at last found surcease, they eyed each other with loathing, with disgust. . . .

Later, after Mimi had left her to her privacy, Leyra closed her eyes and sighed in anguish. Her head drooped against her pillow. As she lay awake and thought over the events of the day, she found that she absolutely could not accept the unheard-of-possibility that stared her straight in the face. Philip had called the doctor for her after all. He had come and gone, telling her that he thought she might be pregnant. Of course he was not sure. Further tests had to be made. She would know in four to six weeks for sure. She just could not absorb the report. Her breath seemed to choke her. She would not breathe even a word of it to anyone—especially to Philip—for what if it should turn out to be untrue?

That night Philip's attempts to make love to her left her unmoved. Her recollection of the various means she had used to stimulate and arouse pleasure in him filled her with disgust and repugnance. With sudden insight she felt sure that their old relationship had died and that they would never again be as they were.

She turned on her side and pretended to sleep in order to evade Philip's groping hands. His breath was warm on the nape of her neck. She pressed her eyes shut tightly together, willing herself to sleep. She tried not to feel the heat that was flowing from him and disgusting her to nausea.

She felt his hands on her thighs, exploring gently. Then his body was pressed close to hers, his legs curled around hers.

"Oh, God!" she prayed, on the verge of screaming out at him, "let him be done with me and go to sleep."

Philip's breathing quickened as his arms tightened about her. After a moment he sighed gently, then released her. She had not moved. She felt him easing away from her and tossing restlessly. He got up softly from the bed and went through the connecting door into Mimi's room. Unexpectedly, blind rage overpowered

Leyra. She lay gripping the sides of the bed as wave after wave of anger ripped and surged through her.

The next morning when Mimi went down to breakfast, Leyra was almost finished with her meal. The two women spoke to each other coldly, though politely. There was a new reserve about Leyra that dampened her usual warmth. Breakfast was a silent meal until Philip joined them.

He bent and kissed his wife on the cheek and pinched her playfully. Mimi was silently toying with a piece of toast.

"Did you sleep well, Mimi? he asked as he seated himself.

"She should have slept well," Leyra observed dryly as she stirred her coffee.

Mimi stared at her curiously. "And why should I have slept well?" she asked. "It was a very hot and muggy night. I tossed and turned until my sheets were practically rag mops. As a matter of fact, I didn't sleep at all. Not that you're really interested."

Leyra's lips twitched. "I wouldn't put it quite like that, if I were you."

"Well, I am sure glad you aren't me!" Mimi said with obvious annoyance.

Leyra flushed scarlet at the implication in the harsh words. Then her face turned ghastly pale. "Just what do you mean by that?" Her voice was barely a whisper.

Philip, almost completely unnerved, tried to change the subject. "Oh, Leyra, dear, I nearly forgot to tell you. I just had a call from the doctor. He wants you to come in for a thorough checkup. Said something about some tests he wants to make, also."

Leyra's hand, holding a table knife, flicked impatiently. "I've already told you that I don't need to see him. I am perfectly all right. The devil with his tests!"

He smiled reassuringly. "Well, dearest, just to please me, please go in to see him anyway. I'd feel so much better."

Mimi got up from the table, tossing her curls that hung down to her shoulders. She had not cut her hair since she became pregnant. Just as she was about to pass Leyra, Leyra's hand flashed out with the knife.

Mimi swerved sharply, but not sharply enough, balked by her heavy body's slowness. A bright red stream gushed out of a cut on her arm.

"Oh! I *am* sorry, darling. Really, I am. That was clumsy of me. Are you hurt badly?"

The concern in Leyra's voice did not match the pleasure mirrored on her face. She quickly wheeled her chair over to Mimi, who was staring at her with complete dismay. Philip was the first to reach Mimi. The sight of the blood had drained his face of color.

"Are you badly hurt?" he asked.

With his help, she walked into the garden. The cut was slight but it bled freely. As Mimi passed her, leaning on Philip's arm, Leyra knew bitter defeat. Philip did not even glance at her as he helped Mimi out of the room into the garden.

During the next few weeks Philip never left Mimi's side, stayed constantly at Forest Green. He was convinced that Leyra had deliberately attempted to injure Mimi. He and Mimi imagined correctly that Leyra's jealousy had at last got the better of her, and they were convinced that she had every intention of harming the unborn child.

Mimi could hardly move and she spent most of her time sitting by the pool, wrapped snugly in a blanket against the occasional crisp autumn day, or in a deck chair on the glass-enclosed porch. The shocking morning was never referred to again. Mimi was determined to leave Forest Green but Philip dissuaded her, reminding her that she was in no condition to take care of herself.

A temporary truce existed for a short time between the two women. Polite words were spoken that hid the true feelings in their hearts. It took Philip a little while to recover from the shock of seeing his goddess of patience and tact attack Mimi. For the first time he really lost interest in Leyra.

Leyra seethed and her headaches became a daily nuisance. She was writing letters at the old writing desk that had belonged to the Captain. She could see Philip and Mimi on the sun porch every time she glanced up.

Martine, the old and withered housekeeper who had been with Leyra's mother, passed by, carrying a tray with two glasses and an iced pitcher. Leyra looked up.

"Is that iced orange juice for Mimi?" she asked.

Martine opened her thin lips that were constantly compressed these days and nodded mutely. She had already let Leyra know that she did not approve of the goings-on in the household. She was the only one of the servants who dared scold Leyra. They both knew that her devotion to her "Bebe" was complete and that nothing could get her to leave the house—not even this "mess," as she termed the involvement with Mimi.

Leyra started to speak but went back to her writing and Martine passed by. But no sooner had Martine disappeared than Leyra lay down her pen and stared at the couple on the porch. She saw Martine pour out the juice and Philip take the glass from her and hand it. to Mimi. Mimi shook her head but at Philip's insistence she took the glass and sipped the juice slowly.

Mimi's pregnancy had taken her appetite. For months she had been only nibbling at her food and living on orange juice. But she had gained the normal amount of weight and the doctor had reported her condition as excellent.

Leyra watched as Philip urged Mimi to take more of the juice. Togo, her white Persian, rubbed against Leyra and mewed complainingly. He adored his mistress and loved to have her pet him, allowing no one else to touch him. Leyra patted her lap and Togo jumped on her blanketed legs. Whispering to him, she wheeled her chair out to join Philip and Mimi.

For the first time since their childhood, Philip was bored with Leyra. It was as if, having once been on a pedestal, she had committed a sacrilege in showing herself to be mortal like other people. The truth was that Philip felt the need to look up to a woman.

As Leyra joined the group, Togo jumped from her lap to the floor and ran straight to Mimi's legs stretched out on an ottoman. Togo had been Leyra's personal property, and now Mimi was taking even him away from her. Her face mirrored the thought in her heart. Panic showed stark and clear.

Mimi knew that she would sooner or later have a real showdown with Leyra, and she cursed herself for having agreed to go through with the mad plan of having Leyra's child for her. The following days seemed endless to Mimi as they dragged into tortured weeks. The strained relationship was always threatening to erupt in actual violence—for Leyra was a soul in torment.

One moment she was in the kitchen fussing with the cook, supervising the preparation of an unusual delicacy for Mimi which she would serve her humbly, prodding her to eat it.

"Now, darling, you must try some of this. It is really yummy and, besides," she would smile her old, winning smile, "you know you need to eat. You're eating for two now, remember."

At such times Mimi would forget the jealous tirades, until Leyra would viciously attack her in the next hour.

"It is really pitiful and pathetic," Mimi said to Philip one day. She had taken to knitting although she did it rather badly. She had been working on the same sweater for months and wondered if she would ever finish it before the baby arrived. Leyra had taught her how to knit long before their relationship had become so twisted.

Philip's lips pursed and the vein in his temple throbbed but he said nothing. Never had Mimi heard him say anything derogatory about Leyra. She smiled ruefully. Her hunger for Griff had become a chronic ache—always with her. It had been ages since he had come out to Forest Green to visit her. She was beginning to worry about it. Was he forgetting her? She half made up her mind to have the chauffeur drive her to the Club the following day.

She felt the child stirring, moving forcefully. He is going to be a strong child, she thought. It was now only a matter of weeks before the baby's birth. Lately she had taken to wondering what it would be like if she and Griff and the baby—had it been Griff's child—were to settle down somewhere. But she knew that that was impossible. Griff was planning on the money to get them started. She and Griff could always have a child when they were ready for one.

The day was crisp and cool. A hint of frost was in the air and she restlessly put down the knitting and stood unsteadily on her feet. As she stood up, she swayed a little and Philip quickly rose to steady her. They stood quietly for a moment, close together. Leyra, wheeling her chair out of the door, saw the pose and stared at them. She was growing increasingly fretful with each passing day. With Mimi's lying-in time nearing Leyra found herself becoming unbearably nervous. Confined to her wheelchair, she had no way of physically working off her excess tension and, as a result, she became increasingly disagreeable. Martine went about her business with pursed lips, silent disapproval registered in every furrow and line of her ancient face.

As Leyra approached the couple, Mimi released herself and walked toward a clump of shrubbery beside the pool. The pool had been drained at the end of summer. She remembered her first night at Forest Green when some too-jolly reveler had chased her and she had concealed herself behind this same shrub. She fingered a leaf absently. How much had happened to her since then! Suddenly someone grasped her waist and spun her half around. Leyra was beside her, her eyes blazing furiously.

"I saw you and Philip just then. It's indecent. Positively indecent, I tell you. The way you two behave—the way you treat me, right in my own house!"

Her voice had risen and she was nearly screaming. Mimi looked around but Philip had disappeared. She was hemmed in by the clump of shrubbery on one side and Leyra and the empty pool on the other. She tried to beat a retreat but she had nowhere to go. She stood facing Leyra uncertainly, a weak smile on her face.

Leyra was in a frenzy. All sanity seemed to have left her. She smiled gloatingly.

"I've got you this time, and Philip—my husband," she emphasized the pronoun, "isn't here to defend you. And you in your condition, and me in this chair, we are even."

There was a cruel, unnatural gleam in her eye that sent shivers of fear up and down Mimi's back—not for herself but for the child she had carried so long.

"Now, look, Leyra! Why don't we sit down for once and talk this thing out like two women?" she asked. "You know this was all your idea. I wanted no part of it. You asked for this," she said firmly.

"Yes, I asked you to have our baby. But I didn't ask you to steal my husband, my man, away from me. And that's what you've been doing."

As she spoke she wheeled her chair until it was pressing against Mimi's legs. Mimi had retreated until she was backing into the shrubbery. Behind Leyra was the only escape, a slow decline that led to the boat anchored below in the bay.

Leyra fumbled in her lap robe and pulled out a long kitchen carving knife. Mimi's eyes widened with alarm and dismay. She had not suspected that Leyra had taken to carrying a knife. Now what have I let myself in for, she wondered. Then, before she could move or collect herself, Leyra leaned from her chair and slashed at her belly.

"I asked for this child but now I don't want it. And you're not going to have it either," she screamed. Again and again she stabbed at Mimi, who clumsily tried to ward off the blows with her arms.

The sleeves of her sweater were gashed and torn and hung in strips. Her arm was cut and bleeding in many places. Her awkwardness was helping the distraught woman. Mimi knew that it was only a matter of time before one of the vicious slashes would land, and suddenly fear gave her added strength. She fought desperately. She clutched Leyra's sleeve and held on. Leyra fought to free herself. She struggled like a mad woman and struck Mimi again and again with her free hand.

Somehow in the struggle the wheelchair brake was released. Before Mimi could grasp what was happening, Leyra and the wheelchair were careening crazily backward, speeding down the slope leading to the bay.

Mimi, gasping for breath, held her bleeding arm. She stared, dumb with shock at the wheelchair dashing down the hill. The chair twisted and turned on its descent. It struck an obstruction on the lawn, spun around, turned over and collapsed on its side. Leyra was thrown to the ground and fell at the base of a tree.

She lay very still. Mimi watched in a trance as Philip tore out of the house and ran toward his wife. Mimi knew that Leyra was dead—killed by a blow on her head as she struck the tree. And she, Mimi, had killed her. Suddenly she gave a moan and bent nearly double as a hot stab of pain wound around her back and belly.

Cold perspiration ran down her face. Again and again the excruciating pain hit her, searing into her very vitals. Her back felt as if pincers were tearing it apart. She was soaked to the skin in a matter of seconds.

She had to get to Griff to tell him she had killed Leyra. But she couldn't think right for the pain. The baby! She was going to have the baby!

"Griff! Oh, Griff!" She staggered toward the garage and turned on the ignition key of the convertible which she always drove. She stepped down hard on the accelerator, backed out of the garage and roared down the curving driveway. She drove automatically, careening down the highway in a crazy, zig-zag course.

She sped through red lights, skidded at sharp curves, the tires squealing. With every second the pain belabored her, blotting out for brief flashes at a time all consciousness. She came to, once, just in time to avoid crashing head on into an embankment.

Another time she didn't come to until the car had bumped its way across a narrow ditch and skidded to a stop in a soggy field. She was pitched forward across the steering wheel. Her eyes were glazed. Blood covered the seat and the floor was wet with it. Only the need to get to Griff kept her alive. She didn't know how badly hurt she was but she knew she had to see Griff. She backed out to the highway and, half-blinded with pain, doggedly careened toward the Club.

TEN

SUDDENLY lights beckoned to her. The car screeched up to the rear door of the Club. She staggered out. Noises were buzzing in her head. Her legs felt like rubber. She headed for the lower floors and the rehearsal rooms. Griff would be working at the piano. She had killed Leyra. She had to see Griff.

It had been months since Mimi had visited the Club. She knew the rehearsal room where Griff usually worked. It had been redecorated. The heavy trappings and ornate wall hangings were gone. Only a Hollywood bed, a work table and a couple of chairs beside the massive piano were left in it.

Mimi staggered down the hall on her way to Griff. She was near unconsciousness and a dreadful sight. Her sweater was in shreds and soggy with blood—some of which had already encrusted. She had torn her bra. Creamy portions of her skin showed through the torn places on her sweater.

She came to the door and stood swaying before it uncertainly. Then she opened it and stood there, groggy and unfocusing as a wave of dizziness hit her. She stared blankly. There were two persons in the room—Griff and Silky. They were lying side by side on the divan, arms entwined about each other.

She had interrupted them in an intimate moment. She stared at them uncomprehendingly. Then she made a slight sound and Griff turned his head. He looked at her dully for a long moment. Then, shaking his head like a wet dog, he waved his hand in her direction and laid his head down again, ignoring her completely. Silky did not even bother to look up. He reached over and pulled

Griff toward him and whispered something in his ear. Mimi heard him giggle.

She called Griff's name. "Griff! Oh, Griff!" Her voice broke hoarsely. She took tottering steps into the room in the direction of the bed.

Silky turned and stared at her. Hatred distorted his face. He sprang from the bed and rushed toward her. He slapped her face twice with both hands and, gripping her by her shoulders, hustled her out of the room and slammed the door behind her. Mimi fell in a crumpled heap outside the door and blackness overcame her.

When she came to consciousness again, she was lying on an ornate bed and her glazed eyes faintly recognized Nick's picture symbols. So she was in Nick's bedroom, the inner sanctum itself. She lifted her hand weakly and saw that it was bandaged. Her back still felt as though it was splitting down the middle. It would be ironic if she should have the child right here, right in the Place.

Her baby deserved to be born in a more respectable place than the Paradise Club, she wept. She tried to sit up. Strong hands forced her back on the pillows. She had not been aware that some- one else was in the room. She opened her eyes again and looked directly into Nick's eyes. They were smiling kindly in the ugly mask of his face. The lines of lust and cruelty were softened.

"Take it easy, kid."

She eyed him. He stared back. As he looked, a slow flush mounted his face until he looked like a big, round, sardonic beet. A beet with wavy black hair and long roots. The roots were Bothio's body. I am having hallucinations, she thought, and made another effort to sit up in bed.

But Nick sat on the side of her bed. Something about his face puzzled her. Was that a tear that rolled down his cheek? As she looked, he fell to his knees beside the bed. His shoulders shook. He was crying! But why?

She wanted to ask him but she could not. He raised a ravaged face to hers. "I am the great Nick Bothio. Men fear me. I destroy them like flies if they get in my way. But here I am kneeling at your feet. Isn't that something? Nick Bothio kneeling at the feet of a small chit of a babe!" The soft voice stopped and the room was very still. "Know why?" he continued. "Because I've always wanted a son. A son! A living, breathing part of me that would be respectable and decent, who could walk straight and proud before all the bastards who look down on me!"

His hand with the slender, elegant fingers reached out and gently stroked her stomach. "And here you are. Sweet and true, carrying a child for a no-good bastard"—he stood up and began pacing the floor—"who's fooling around with that fruit!"

Mimi tried to protest. Her voice rasped feebly. She still could not believe what she had seen. "It's not true. He isn't!" she murmured. Then her foggy mind realized that Nick did not know of the deal with the Thorntons. He thinks this is Griff's baby. She started to laugh.

Nick stared at her. "What's funny?"

"Nothing," she gasped. Nick did not know she was close to having the baby right in his room. She started to tell him but then he bent over her and his fingers traced a tender, delicate pattern on her face.

She cringed away from him. He mistook the action for fear. "Don't be afraid," he murmured. "I'm not going to hurt you. You reach the soft part of me, kid."

He looked at her but he was not seeing her. He was talking more to himself than to her. "Every man has a weakness, they say. Yeah. That's right. And a pregnant woman is mine." His eyes focused on her. "I've always been weak for you, though. I thought you could do for me what no other woman has ever been able to do." He cradled her face in his two hands. "I've wanted you for so long. I waited because I thought you loved that bum. I wanted you so bad that fires burned in me."

Mimi looked toward the door and saw Asia standing as if rooted to the spot.

"Asia," she whispered, but Nick cut her off.

"Asia? I've never loved Asia. I picked her up in a Paris gutter. A kid. I felt sorry for her and she has her place. But you—" A tornado lived and breathed in his eyes. "I'll get you to a hospital, kid, and when this is over, you, me and the kid are going away somewhere—anywhere—South America perhaps, and live like respectable people. Yeah! I'll adopt the kid. We'll make it."

"Asia." Again Mimi could only whisper the name.

"Damn Asia! I was getting tired of her anyway. As for that musician, I'll kill the sonuvabitch. When he hurts you, baby, he's squeezing my guts."

His face was savage and wild, a grotesque distorted mask. He means it, she thought. "No! Don't hurt him. I love him. Please, Nick."

She clung to his hand as he turned to leave. He loosened her feeble hold and strode out of the room. Mimi forced herself out of the bed, fighting against the numbing pain that tore her body into a million sparks of stabbing fire.

She had to get to Griff before Nick did and warn him. She had to get him to understand. She got to her feet but a sickening flash of agony shook her. She reeled and, groaning, fell in a heap on the floor. In a minute the fiery attack passed, leaving only a hot ache, and she dragged herself along the carpet. Inch by inch she pulled herself.

She had to get to Griff. She knew with finality that Bothio was going to kill him. She had never seen the mobster filled with such deadly purposefulness. Her woman's instinct made her sure. When she reached the door, she could go no further. Another wave of excruciating torture descended upon her. She bent over, clutching her knees as her whole body was bathed in a cold sweat.

"Oh, dear God. Let me get to him," she prayed from the depths of her being. But even as her lips moved in the silent prayer, blackness overcame her and she lay motionless, a crumpled, unconscious heap at the foot of the door.

ELEVEN

WHEN Nick Bothio strode out of the room with murder in his heart for Griff, he did not know that forces were already working against him and that he would soon be involved in a titanic struggle for his own life.

Mimi had not been able to tell him that she had seen Asia at the door. So, unaware that the dancer, insane with fury, had turned against him, Bothio headed for the rehearsal room where Griff and Silky kept their rendezvous.

Asia had had enough time to get there before him. Time to set in motion forces which would destroy Nick Bothio and the empire he had built with his strength and life's blood. She, Asia, with a woman's acute prescience, had long sensed the change in her lover. That he had been attracted to Mimi she had known from the first.

That Nick wanted a son desperately, she knew also. It had been a tremendous disappointment for Nick that she had never become pregnant for him. As time passed, she had hoped that it would happen for then the child would be her insurance against being thrown off by Nick for another woman. But the child never came.

And now he was planning this. Well, she would see about it! She rushed to the rehearsal room. Griff was in the state of semi-drunkenness that had become his habit since Silky had taken possession of "his soul," as he put it.

Silky, however, never allowed himself to lose control of his own faculties. He was cold sober. Silky, an enigma to all but a psychiatrist, was a combination of contradictions. Beneath the soft, feminine ways and the make-up was a shrewd mind that worked constantly to Silky's advantage. This, backed by strong, dextrous muscles and a special gift with the silken cord, had kept him close to the top of gangdom's aristocracy. He was cunning and ruthless.

As Asia burst into the room, wild-eyed with the news that Bothio was about to ditch Griff on the wayside and make off with Mimi and her baby, Silky saw the chance he had been waiting for for years. The dormant lust to kill that was part of the crooked skein of his personality rose to the surface.

He and Asia hatched a plan that was to become bloody history recorded in the city's crime archives. Sitting on the side of the bed, his legs swinging nonchalantly, the unmanly creature listened quietly without interrupting the dancer's story. His chest heaved and his fingers flexed and coiled. These and the burning in the limpid eyes were the only signs that he was disturbed by the tale the trembling girl brought.

"I'm not going to let him get away from me," Asia was whispering sibilantly. Her Chinese accent became marked under stress. "He's not going away with her!"

"He's not going anywhere!" Silky answered slowly. "This day has been coming for a long time. And I am ready for it."

"What are you going to do?" the girl asked, frightened.

"Baby doll, this town is gonna see some fireworks like it's never seen before!" the other answered grimly. "And while we are at it, I'll take care of the girl, too."

A strange fire burned in Silky's eyes. Asia turned cold. She had not meant for either Nick or Mimi to be hurt. She had wanted only to keep Nick from going away with Mimi.

"You aren't going to hurt her?" she asked, ashen-faced. "She's going to have the child in any minute. I can tell. She's in labor right now."

"That's fine. We'll help it along a little. Then—bingo!" His fingers snapped and, like a flash, the silken cord appeared from nowhere, a thin, white tendril, curling and twisting. Asia hissed through her teeth and cringed in fear.

The man was a maniac. What had she done in her fit of jealousy? But it was too late now to stop him. She could not handle this monster with the grinning leer that contorted his features into the countenance of absolute evil.

"Now listen! This is the set-up. Nick is expecting a huge shipment of the white stuff on a ship coming in today. Who do you think is slated to pick it up from the sailor that's bringing it in?"

Asia tried to move her stiff lips but they would not obey. She pointed a finger and nodded toward him.

"You?"

"That's right on the ball, kid. Me." A wicked chortle escaped his slender throat. "There'll be a surprise on the dock today for the great Nick Bothio."

There was such wickedness in the chuckle that Asia turned to ice. She did not want Nick killed. She loved him! "You're not planning on killing him, Silky, are you?" She had to force the words out. This was a madman. She had made a horrible mistake in coming to him.

"It's *been* time for a change around here, baby," the henchman answered grimly. "I've been playing it cool and waiting and watching a long time for this one, just one little slip by the great Nick B. And here it is!"

He smacked his fist into a palm and jumped to his feet as lithely as a cat. Asia clung to him tightly, sobbing wildly.

"But you can't kill him. You can't. I love him. I want him alive!"

Silky looked down at her from his height and smiled wickedly. "You're way out of line now, baby. You should've thought of this before. Women! You love him so you betray him." The contempt in his voice was vile. He pushed her away from him roughly. "Let go of me. Bitch!"

He turned to Griff who was asleep on the bed. With a delicate, feminine motion, he bent and tenderly stroked Griff's flaccid face. Asia, weeping inconsolably, crept from the room. This was not the way she had wanted things to go. She did not know yet how she would stop him, but Bothio was not going to be killed by this perverted monster.

Silky let her go. He was confident that she would not risk death by revealing his plans to Bothio—and thus revealing her own treachery.

After she left the room, Silky continued stroking Griff's face. He talked softly to himself as if the sleeping man could hear him.

"Now you sleep tight, honey. I have a few things to attend to but I'll be back soon. Then we'll see who's boss around here! That boat should be coming in just about now. And I have a date with a sailor and a gang of gunmen. But first, I must make a phone call."

As Asia stumbled out of the rehearsal room, eyes brimming with tears, she bumped into Bothio in the hall on his way to find Griff. He pushed her aside roughly. She clung to him.

The past hour had made changes in Asia. Her face was swollen and her eyes were puffy. Her skin had an unusually sallow cast.

"Let me go, Asia. I've got business with that no-good bum in there," Nick growled.

"No! No! You can't go in there," Asia screamed at him, pulling him back. "He'll kill you. He's waiting for you."

Nick stopped in his tracks and stared at her. "What? Who's waiting? Griff?"

Asia shook her head. "No, Silky! He's planning on taking over the organization. He's been double-crossing you, Nick. I didn't want him to—just to get rid of Mimi but—but—" She burst into a fresh flood of tears.

Bothio seized her arm roughly. "Talk! What's going on? What's Silky up to?"

Asia, sick at heart, stammered the story through her tears. Nick listened without interrupting, his face a grotesque mask. At last she was silent.

"So Silky thinks he can pull the double-cross and take over from me, eh? Why, of all the rotten, goddam nerve. I'll kill him with my bare hands."

He paced up and down the hall like a wild animal, pulling at his shirt cuffs, screaming at the top of his voice. "Ha! We'll see about that. That pansy has his nerve. I'll have a surprise or two for this doublecrossing rat."

He picked up a chair and hurled it against the opposite wall where it broke into pieces and scattered over the carpet. His face was convulsed and almost purple. Then, just as suddenly, his anger gave way to a cold restraint that frightened Asia even more.

Bothio sat quite still, unmoving, like a wooden carving. At last he stirred and smiled a cruel smile. "We'll take care of that punk."

He got up and, without another word, went out. Asia sat cowering where he left her. Her world was crumbling about her and she herself had helped to pull down the foundation.

Once more Sal, Crappo, The Greek and their cohorts, all gangdom's elite, were gathered around a conference table. The meeting room differed vastly from Nick's conference room. All present had responded to a hurry-up call by Sal and were seated in the backroom of The Greek's pool parlor.

There was a deadly purposefulness about the meeting. Each knew from the grapevine why he had been called. There was only one item on the agenda. Nick Bothio. *Stop Nick Bothio!*

Sal was the chairman. He went right to the issue. "Well, what are ya guys gonna do about Bothio? I did everything possible to avoid a showdown at this time. You all know this. I told him we couldn't afford notice now from the Fed boys."

"Nick must be nuts!" somebody exclaimed.

"Yeah, but no one of us is big enough to fight us all together," The Greek growled, chomping on his unlit cigar. He shifted his cigar to the other side of his mouth. "We took care of the Weasel the way we said. The Weasel promised to lay off him. So he should of left the Weasel alone."

"Yeah. But are you sure what you heard is true?" Crappo asked. "I think we oughta check with Bothio first." Crappo was the ugliest man in the room. His eyes popped out of his head and his abnormally long arms reached to the floor, hanging loosely from his sides over the case he was sitting on.

There was a stillness following his statement. Then Sal spoke again. "We don't need to check. It's true enough. Silky himself called me."

"Something stinks!" Crappo insisted. "I don't trust that queer. Why should Silky play stoolie against his boss?"

"I've already told you that, too, Crappo. Stop objecting! If you don't want in, then stay out. Nobody is twisting your arm. But I'll tell you once again. Silky said Nick is planning to skip the country with the doll of that musician of his. So c'mon, ya mugs. We'll take a vote. We've had enough talk. We all know what it's all about."

Sal looked around the room and gazed in every man's face. "All for ganging up against Bothio where he's supposed to meat the Weasel, say 'aye.' " There was an overwhelming chorus of ayes.

"Boss, why did they chose the docks?" somebody asked.

" 'Choose,' ya lunkhead! That was real cute of Bothio. The Weasel has a fish concession there and he's expecting an early shipment of fish this evening—before the other boats get in. So Nick thinks up a hot surprise. Well, will he be the surprised one!"

"Will the Weasel be there, too, Sal? After all, this is his fight!"

"Of course he'll be there. He'd better. We'll be there, too."

There was silence in the room as each of the men thought of the plot to curb Bothio or—perhaps—eliminate him.

The sun had gone down and mothers had already wheeled their babies home as Silky walked leisurely along the quiet waterfront. It had been a beautiful day in the city. It was going to be an exciting night.

Along the river motorboats cruised lazily, leaving white riffs in their wakes. Silky had driven to the city from the Club and parked near the United Nations building. As he walked down the East River Drive to Thirtieth Street, he stopped now and then and looked at the river. Actually, he was looking for a rowboat that was supposed to meet him further down. He wanted to see it before the man in the boat glimpsed him.

But the river was free of rowboats. He stopped a cab. "Down the Drive! I'll tell you when to stop!" he told the cabbie.

"Right!" the cabbie started off. They drove down the Drive until they came to Catherine Slip. "Stop here!" Silky ordered.

He got out and walked over toward the fishmarkets. It was dark, but not dark enough. He looked at his watch. He had time to kill. The neighborhood in the daytime bustled with jostling people. It was an area of packing houses for the nearby fishmarkets. On the water side of the street a few boats were tied to the pier.

About two blocks distant were the fishmarkets. Their stench gave a distinctive aroma to the area. A few hours hence these markets would be humming with activity as ships unloaded their cargoes of fish.

Now the market was silent, the doors locked and bolted. Across from the market were huge warehouses. An all-night restaurant did a sluggish business while waiting for the boats to dock.

The light from the restaurant streamed onto the sidewalk. Inside were a couple of stragglers and a news-hawk from the daily journal that had its offices a few blocks away. No one moved on the. street. It was a good neighborhood to be out of after dark.

The stage was set. The actors knew their parts. The play would go on and Nick Bothio was the star.

Silky looked at his watch. He had time to kill. Pietro, the Italian cook, was not due until nine o'clock. In the distance the large hulk of a ship riding anchor stood out sharply in the gloom.

Silky walked over to a ramshackle pier near the water. He sat on one of the wooden piles and waited and watched the water. Music from the juke box in the restaurant reached him faintly. It was a long time before he heard a slap, slap in the water.

It was very faint, so faint that he had to strain to hear it. He sat perfectly still, as tense as a cat, waiting. This was going to be it. A thin smile curled his lips. His hand curled and uncurled rhythmically. Inside his curled left fist buried deep in his pocket was the silken cord. It felt good against his palm. He carried a gun, a somewhat womanish .32, but it was the cord that gave him that feeling of assurance. Then he heard a faint movement on the water. A vague, shadowy blur could be seen. As he strained his eager eyes in the darkness, a tall figure mounted the piling.

Silky gave a low chuckle of relief. "Thought you were never gonna make it, man."

"Had to wait my chance, bub. Can't just slip off the ship with this stuff. It's hot. There's about five million dollars here," the man patted his chest, "when it's watered down. Even so, I'm right on time."

"Yeah. Yeah. I guess you're right, man. Give it here!"

"Not so fast. How do I know you're the one?"

The man reached into his coat and drew out an oilskin-wrapped package.

"Who else knew where and when to meet you?" Silky asked. Then, as the other still hesitated, "Got any better suggestions than your ten per cent?"

At the mention of his cut, the man breathed easy. He fumbled in his coat again and came up with a paper bag. "Got a butt, huh? I left mine on the ship."

"Sure, Here!" Silky's left fist dug into his pocket and then reached out to the man. Like a flash the silk cord was tight about the man's throat. "A butt isn't what you really need, is it, bub?" He grinned as he pulled the cord tighter and tighter. He could feel it cutting, penetrating deep into the soft flesh of the neck as the man sank to his knees.

He pulled the .32 and mercilessly gun-whipped the sailor's head. The gurglings and struggles ceased and the lifeless form slid to the pier. Silky looked around. No one was in sight.

He deftly dragged the dead man to the edge of the pier and heaved him over the side. The body made a light splash. Casually Silky sauntered away from the pier. He walked faster as he neared the restaurant.

"Jeez! I am going to be rich. Really rich. For the first time in my life, I am going to be top guy." He was so carried away by his thoughts that he didn't hear the footsteps behind him until the voice spoke.

"That's far enough, Silky. Pass it over! Quick! And don't try anything or you are dead, man. Real dead."

Silky froze in his tracks. Bothio! How had he known? Asia! Sure, the doll. He should have killed her. His first mistake. He would take care of her later.

"Hi, Nick! Didn't expect to find you playing bodyguard for me. Good deal."

"Yeah. Hand it over! You dirty, double-crossing rat. I'd love to give it to you right here."

"You're not Nick!" Silky began sweating.

"Never said I was. I'm Crappo. Not that it's going to do You any good."

If only Crappo were in front of him. But he had no chance to use either his cord or his gun. His mind groped for a way out. Even as he thought, Crappo reached over and took the gun from its holster. Now he had only the cord in his hip pocket, still wet and soggy.

"Listen, Crappo! Let's make a deal. There's plenty here, man. Plenty for everybody. The way things look, nobody else is coming out alive. So let's split it, what do you say? Straight down the middle. You and me. They'd never suspect."

He waited. The other man laughed. "You dirty, double-crossing rat! I ought to let you have it right now."

Crappo's groping hand found the oilskin-wrapped package. Silky relaxed a little. The stuff was in the paper bag. The gun jabbed viciously in his back.

"Nobody knows I've got the stuff. Jake was supposed to pick it up as usual."

"Yeah? Where's Jake now, pal? He couldn't pick up the stuff, even if he wanted to, could he?" The gun jabbed him again, hard. "I'll tell you why he couldn't. Because you gave poor old Jake the business. That's why! We found him right where you left him, strangled! You're the louse who's been tipping the Weasel all along!"

A car was cruising slowly behind them. A gunshot exploded into the quiet night. Crappo jerked at the sudden sound. He had expected it from down the street, but the car was coming from the north, behind him.

The Weasel and Sal and the boys were down at the south end of the market. He turned his head ever so slightly. It was enough for Silky. At the sound of the gunshot, he had frozen in place. Now he eased his head around. Crappo's head was turned as he listened in the night. Silky pivoted on his toes like a ballet dancer. His right fist flashed out with a right uppercut to Crappo's chin. His left fist landed low under the belly. "That's all from you, joker! You talk too much."

Crappo doubled but still managed to hold on to his gun. Before he could straighten up, Silky had dropped the still damp cord about his neck. Crappo fell in a limp heap. Removing the cord with swift dexterity, Silky groped for his .32 and the oilskin decoy and hurried away into the darkness of the markets.

The fishmarkets were a row of one-story buildings along the river side of the street. Fronting the buildings was one long, common wooden platform and one huge, wooden door that slid out of view when it was opened. The buildings faced on the river so the fishing boats could dock easily with their bows in each market.

There were no windows in the middle buildings. Silky crawled along the length of the market until he came to the last building on the north side. Here he broke a window and climbed over the sill. He dropped lithely on the long loading platform in the rear of the markets. The river slurped at his feet as he carefully picked his way along.

Suddenly he stopped. Ahead voices whispered furtively. He saw vague shadows moving about in a boat tied to the dock some yards away. The Weasel! Unloading his stuff from across the river.

The heroin burned a hole in Silky's pocket. After the reception he had had from Crappo, he could not bet on any friendship from Sal's men. He backed up until he came to a door that gave a little. He applied his weight and forced the door. It gave. He entered cautiously.

There was just one big room with weighing bins and bushel baskets hanging from nails on the walls. The smell of fish was overpowering. He bumped into a pile of baskets on the floor and tripped. He sprawled on the concrete floor. A stabbing pain shot through his ankle. "Damn!" he swore. The door to the street was facing him. He got to his feet, hobbled to it and pulled at the wooden plank that was against it. The plank held fast.

He applied all of his weight against it and pulled again. It moved a fraction of an inch. He looked around and saw a grappling hook used for grappling baskets of fish from the boats. With this he finally moved the plank and the door slid back on its hinges easily.

He looked out cautiously. He was in the middle of the row of market buildings. To his left he heard a muffled curse.

He crouched to the floor. Then from the right a shot reverberated loudly in the quiet street. As he watched, a shadowy form appeared and stood like a dark pillar in the night.

"C'mon out, you guys! C'mon out and fight like men. I'll take on any of ya!"

It was Nick Bothio. In spite of himself, Silky grinned. Nick had nerve. Taking on the whole Combo. He knew the jig was up for him but he would never stop fighting—not as long as he could draw a breath.

A burst of machine-gun fire strafed the night. When the firing ceased, there was a deathly silence. Nick had been answered. Suddenly pandemonium broke loose. Someone yelled, "Let the bastards have it!" Bullets flew like flying saucers in front of Silky. A noise behind him made him freeze. Someone was on the platform on the river side. He whirled and, moving as fast as he could on his wrenched ankle, made for the landing platform.

Three boats had silently eased up to the docks while the shooting had been taking place out front. He could see shadowy forms standing in the boats as they pulled up. Then they weren't shadows any more. He could see them clearly. There were men as thick as flies crouching on the platform behind Sal and his group. Bothio's men!

Silky, crouching in the dark, smiled grimly at the cleverness of Nick's plan. The shooting out front was just a decoy. The real fighting was back here. He would not take bets on how many would get out of the trap.

He started easing himself back the way he had come. He wanted out. Safety was his play. He had some unfinished business to attend to. Instead of going out the door as he had entered, he followed the end wall of the market to where there was a clump of tall weeds in a patch used for refuse cans.

Once there he would be safe. He could sprint for the rest of the way and then melt in with the pedestrians a couple of blocks further up. He was about to turn the corner when he bumped, head-on, into somebody coming fast from the opposite way.

"Omph!" The wind was knocked out of him. The other gave a gasp, more of surprise than discomfort. A quick fist grazed Silky's ear, and his .32 belched angry fire.

"You goddam pansy!" Nick! It was Nick himself!

Instead of straightening up, Silky dug in with his toes and drove with his head down, straight for the other's belly. He heard a grunt as he connected. He twisted his body and flipped to the side, grabbing Nick's legs as he turned.

Nick sprawled on the concrete floor. Silky heard the clink of metal as Nick's gun slid out of his hand to the floor. Nick rolled over once and his groping hand felt air. He was on the brink of the loading platform. Below, the river waters slapped and the abyss yawned coldly.

Silky dropped his body down and clung to the platform by his fingers, hoping that Nick could not see any better than he could in the dark. Then he heard running footsteps disappearing toward the shooting.

They were clobbering each other. Well, let 'em! He was heading for safety. He clambered up and ran in a crouch, his sprained ankle forgotten but sending shooting pains up his leg.

Luck was with him. He spied Nick's car parked at the edge of the parking lot. The motor was running. He got in and gunned it and roared off fast. Ahead of him a police siren gave a strident warning. He turned left into a westbound street. Let them go, he thought, settling down for the ride to the Club. He didn't know how seriously he had hurt Nick but he knew the bullet had struck him. He wondered how many would live to talk about the night.

TWELVE

GRIFF was dreaming that he was on a boat sailing in soft clouds that parted mysteriously as he neared them. He could see Mimi clearly as she stood in her nude loveliness with the clouds enveloping her.

Suddenly the boat began to rock. He was terrified lest it would capsize. He stretched out his hand to Mimi, who was calling him, but each time he touched her fingers, the boat rocked and he would miss her clutching hand. He tossed his head from side to side on the pillow. Then instantly he was wide awake.

Someone was calling him and shaking him by his shoulder. He could not register at first. He sat up in bed, holding his head. Christ! What a hangover he always had.

"Griff! You must do something! They are all mad. And Mimi has to get to a hospital or she will die. She's been in labor all day."

Griff stared at Asia. The dancer was a shocking sight. Her face was swollen and blotchy. Her clothes were torn and in disarray. Her blouse had been ripped from her shoulders and hung by one sleeve. There were bruises on her shoulders and neck, and one eye was turning dark blue.

"What happened?" he asked, heading for the washstand. As he doused his head and face, she told him. Then, with one leap he bounded through the door and down the hall into Bothio's room. Mimi was still on the floor where Asia had left her. The dancer had placed a pillow under Mimi's head but had not been able to lift her to the bed.

Mimi was in a coma from shock and pain. The child had been vainly seeking its way out for hours. She lay in a twisted heap. Her face was a white mask. She was cold and clammy to Griff's touch.

At sight of the pitiful heap on the floor, the two years of their life together flooded over Griff with full force. He knew bitter remorse. Shame and self-loathing weighed on him.

He bent down and picked Mimi up and laid her on the bed. He sat beside her and cradled her head in his lap. Asia pulled at his arm hysterically.

"Griff, you must get her to a hospital. Griff! Griff! There's not time."

But contrition and guilt made him powerless. He gently wiped the dampness from Mimi's face. "Oh, baby, I'm so ashamed! Forgive me. Please baby, forgive me. I'm no good but I love you! I do."

He laid his head against the mass of her hair and wept unashamedly. "We'll go away together, baby. Just as we planned. You'll see. We'll go away."

Mimi opened her eyes and looked at him. "Griff? I knew you would come," she said feebly. She moaned and moved restlessly.

"It's me, baby. Your Griff. Don't worry about anything. You'll be all right. Then when you're better—you and me, we're going away."

From the doorway a voice spoke insolently. "You're going away all right. But not with her. You're going away with me, baby."

Silky entered the room. He towered over them, death and desperation etched on his face, furrowing the once-smooth cheeks. His eyes were burning, wild pits. His make-up had smeared and his hair hung in dank wisps over his brow. Asia cringed against the head of the bed. Silky laughed grimly. With a sudden, threatening gesture, he pointed his gun at the terrified girl. "You ratted on me, doll. You won't live to talk about it."

His voice rose to a screaming falsetto. He raised the gun until it pointed straight to her heart. His hand shook with passion. His face was distorted with hate as he walked toward her. Then, with a sudden contemptuous motion, he flipped the gun out of his hand. It slithered to the opposite side of the room.

"This I want to do with my own bare hands!" he gritted hoarsely. Asia raised her frightened face to him beseechingly. She was petrified with fear. Just as his hand was about to touch her, she galvanized into life, and bolted to the door, screaming wildly.

At the door, a dirty and disheveled figure blocked her path. Asia's scream ended in mid-cry. Nick Bothio stood there. His left arm hung limply at his side. He had lost his tie and his coat was torn and rumpled. There was the stench of blood about him and the look of death in his eyes. His grotesque face was a frozen mask, almost beautiful in its granite resoluteness. He looked at Asia dispassionately.

"Hi ya, kid," he said softly. His voice was devoid of emotion, cold and implacable. Asia, sobbing wildly, entwined her arms about his neck and would have kissed his mouth but he held himself aloof. Her lips brushed his bruised cheek.

Then, while she clung close to him, he raised the gun to her side. There was a sharp click in the room. His arm lowered slowly as Asia's body fell in a heap at his feet.

"You were mine, doll—but you forgot and pulled the double-cross. Now you know," he whispered.

Silky fell to his hands and knees, searching frantically for the gun he had tossed away. Nick's eyes were glazed and his mouth was twisted into a cruel sneer.

"You're dead, rat. Even if you find it!"

He raised his gun and leveled it at the strangler. Silky whirled up from his crouch and came at a dead run from across the room. He yanked up a chair just as the bullet sang past his arm, tearing his coat sleeve. He tossed the chair. Nick side-stepped it. But Silky and the chair were in motion at the same time. Nick's side-step had brought him in line with Silky's moving body and he felt the crushing impact of Silky's fist. His head snapped back from the straight uppercut Silky flushed on his chin. His eyes darkened and he weaved back a step. The next moment he had closed in on Silky, who was trying to grab his throat.

Bothio pulled the trigger of his gun just as Silky's deadly cord coiled itself around his opponent's neck. Silky's fingers tightened convulsively, completing the twist-knot locking the cruel loop. The gun spoke again. The fingers held.

At last, with a choking, gurgling sound, Nick slackened. His knees buckled. He and Silky went down together, held fast to the last in an act of mutual destruction.

Griff gathered Mimi to him and carried her to the elevator that opened to the rear of the Club where the parking lot was located. Nick's car was nearby. Griff placed Mimi on the seat and headed for the open road and a hospital.

Mimi did not appear to be breathing. She was a pale, waxen figure crumpled beside him. Griff never noticed how fast he was driving. He did not notice the car that held to his taillight. He kept his foot down hard on the accelerator as the needle spun crazily.

He could not believe that all that had happened to him and Mimi in the past few months was real. That he had been a borderline case he now knew. His guilt was not for this but for the wasted love Mimi had spent on him. She was a good kid and he knew that in his own way he loved her as much as he could ever love anyone.

His relationship with Silky was clothed in mystery and fuzzy uncertainty. Most of the time he had been too drunk with dope or liquor to know or care what was happening. His degradation was complete. He thought of the bright future he had painted to Mimi for them both. He had thought it a possibility but Fate had had other plans. Well, if this was the way it was to be, than that was it.

He gazed at Mimi again. He knew she was dying. Life without her would be bleak. Theirs had been a strangely beautiful sort of life together. Their need for one another had been great but he knew he had never fulfilled Mimi's true desires. And now he knew why. He could not. He had been true to only one thing in his life, music. Always his best music had come when he was with her. He had not done anything good, anything that he really liked, while she was away.

He turned the wheel sharply and with his right hand reached over and brought Mimi to him. His foot was still down hard on the floorboard. As the car hit the abutment, music ran through his head. It fused in a loud crescendo as pain and blackness blended together in a great symphonic finale.

They were still together when they were thrown from the car. He was dying. Mimi had fallen partly across him. Her face was near his head. He tried to move his body but could not. With a great effort, he turned his head and saw that Mimi's clothing had been torn from her body. One heavy breast was exposed.

He reached forward, using every ounce of will. His lips found and tasted the warmth of the fullness. Cold sweat streamed down his cold face. His fingers groped agonizingly and pulled her dress down, covering the lovely nakedness.

They were found still clasped together, his arm cradling her body. Mimi was rushed to the hospital but she died on the operating table, never recovering consciousness. She did not live to see the beautiful daughter who had survived the ordeal.

Griff was tabbed by an indifferent officer as DOA, dead on arrival. The Paradise Club had not been Paradise for any of them after all.

THIRTEEN

THE NURSE writing on the chart at the desk knew that she was beautiful. Her uniform fitted her like a second skin. It revealed more than it concealed. Her firm young breasts thrust forward invitingly like peaks of fresh ice cream on a hot summer day.

She cast a sly look at Philip under long, curling lashes. All the good-lookers were married. What chance did a pretty nurse have? If he asked her for a date, would he be surprised at how fast she would say yes!

She knew of Philip. Thornton wealth maintained the hospital. She knew of the big estate called Forest Green and imagined a life in it based on romantic movies and sensational tabloids.

She looked squarely at him and caught him staring at her. Had she seen something—a flicker of interest—in the depths of his eyes? In spite of herself, she blushed deep scarlet. Philip hurriedly turned his gaze away. If he had met her sooner, he might have dared challenge the invitation in her eyes.

But now his life was changed. So much had happened since he and Leyra had started out on their quest for a child that he felt like a man returning home after a long, long trip—strange and rather apart.

"She's all right, I'm sure, Mr. Thornton. But Dr. MacDingle will be out to talk to you soon."

Philip smiled. He remembered how lost and afraid he had been when he had bent over Leyra lying so white and still, her legs twisted under her after her wheelchair had crashed down the slope and smashed against the tree. In that first instant he had recognized that his love for Leyra had never died.

As he had held the still form of his wife in his arms, his world had spun about him. Without Leyra, a fundamental part of him would die. She was his strength and his mainstay. The knowledge brought him no shame. He felt relieved, as if his long search was at an end, leaving him purged and empty.

"Mr. Thornton, Dr. MacDingle will see you now." The pretty nurse still smiled an invitation but Philip was unreceptive. She frowned and, turning, walked ahead of him to the doctor's office. Her hips were round and unrestrained under the form-fitting uniform. The motion was gentle, a quiet and yet provocative, rhythmical swaying of the body. His pulse quickened. She held the door open for him and he entered.

The old doctor had been Philip's physician since childhood. He smiled a good-natured reassurance to him. His eyes were as blue as the sky in the summer in his native New England.

"Well, young man. I've got a surprise! Allow me to tell you that you are going to be a father." He waited for the effect of his announcement.

Philip only stared. "What?"

"It will have to be a Caesarean delivery but if she can keep it for even seven months, you will have your heir."

Not after all this! What irony! "Are—are you sure, Dr. MacDingle?" Philip whispered.

The doctor nodded. "Yep! All the tests have been made. She's pregnant, all right!"

"But I can't believe it! We had given up all hope. How is Leyra taking it? Have you told her yet?" he asked.

"I've told her. But I must admit she had me worried for a while. Took it a bit unexpectedly. I don't quite understand why she—. But she's game. She'll be all right. She should have been expecting something because several weeks ago I told her I suspected as much."

"I must see her right away." Philip stood up nervously.

"Er—wait a minute." Dr. MacDingle stopped him. "There's something else. That girl who they brought in almost dead—Mimi-something-or-other. She died during the operation to save the baby. I understand that you and Leyra are to adopt the child. It's the most beautiful baby girl I've ever seen." He stared in space. "The mother was beautiful, too. Must have been in labor for hours. The man was dead when they brought him here. Peculiar position they found him in, too, I hear. He must have loved her a great deal. His last dying act was—an act of love."

Philip fidgeted. The doctor stared at him curiously. "You knew him, too, didn't you?" There was a question lurking in the wise blue eyes. Philip found himself equal to it. No need to go over that story again. It belonged to the past, to Mimi and Griff.

"Yes, I knew them both," he answered, looking directly at the doctor and implying that he would say nothing more about the matter. "The adoption papers have already been signed. Everything will be taken care of but I want to talk to Leyra first. Do you mind if I see her now?"

Philip went down the corridor to Leyra's room. The hospital had a special wing reserved for the Thorntons and their relatives. He found Leyra propped up against a great mound of pillows. She was pale and drawn.

"Hey, you!" she greeted him, using their old, familiar expression. Philip dropped to his knees beside the bed and Leyra's hand reached out to caress him.

"Poor baby! What you've been through with me in the last few months," she said softly. "And now you are going to be a father twice in quick succession."

He raised his head and looked at her. "You know about Mimi and her baby?"

She nodded. "Yes. Through the grapevine—the nurse." Her eyes gazed into space. "You know, Phil, I think that maybe we were so sure that we were never going to have a child of our own that we did wrong. I feel somehow that Mimi's death is all our fault."

"I feel that way, too. God, I feel awful! If only she hadn't run in panic."

"You know, I'm going to teach our son to have more faith than his parents did," she declared.

"Son? How do you know it's going to be a son?"

"I just know," she answered simply, as women have answered foolish men-questions for centuries. "You'll see if it isn't a boy. A wonderful son for his wonderful father to love."

The image of Dr. MacDingle entered Philip's mind suddenly. He hesitated. As if reading his thoughts, Leyra answered his unspoken question. "We are going through with the arrangements we made with Mimi to adopt her baby, aren't we? We can't just let it go away from us. Imagine! Having two children all of a sudden like this!"

Philip looked hard at Leyra. Her face and eyes were sure. A wave of love surged over him. A moan escaped him at the thought that he might have lost her. He felt a sudden overpowering hunger for her and his mouth claimed hers gently. His tongue probed, twisting and turning, darting here and there, gathering in the sweet, delicious nectar as a bee gathers honey from the depths of a flower.

He was all male, demanding and sure of himself as he enfolded her in his arms. Never had he been so masterful. Previously it had always been Leyra who dominated. He now realized the joy of conquering and claiming his fruit from the vine. From now on the initiative would be his—he felt fully male, forceful and strong.

His lips moved reluctantly from her clinging lips to the creamy warmth of her throat. Greedily he nibbled at the velvety softness. He heard Leyra's soft whisperings. She bent over him and her hands, strong but gentle, searched, questing for him. His body quivered. Heaven opened its doors and Leyra's journey was done. His body shuddered and lunged tumultuously and he screamed against her breasts.

THE END

www.ingramcontent.com/pod-product-compliance
Lightning Source LLC
Chambersburg PA
CBHW020913180626
46816CB00007BA/2379